SISTERS FOR VICTORY

The Secret Sirens Series
Book One

D. R. Bailey

SAPERE
BOOKS

SISTERS FOR VICTORY

Published by Sapere Books.

24 Trafalgar Road, Ilkley, LS29 8HH

saperebooks.com

ISBN: 978-0-85495-569-5

I would like to dedicate this book to my two nieces, Anna and Jennifer. Now grown up with families of their own, they have always shown an optimistic resilience to life which could easily pass for wartime spirit. And just like the characters in this series, they both live up to the adage that not all heroines wear capes.

CHAPTER ONE

September 1942
East Sussex, England

I skimmed low across the field and then flew straight up before looping the Tiger Moth with practised ease. Hopefully, it might draw a few admiring gasps from the meagre crowd watching below. I was just coming to the end of my acrobatic performance and for a finale, I intended to drop down in a corkscrew. That always impressed them.

It was a beautiful day in late autumn and the sun shone gloriously across the landscape of our farm. There wasn't a cloud in sight as I gained sufficient height to perform the manoeuvre. It was tricky but the kite started to drop like a stone, just as it always did. This time, though, the engine began to stutter. Damn it… I was going to stall, and then I'd be in the basket.

My heart began to race as I tried to pull the Moth out of the dive. I could feel the engine was about to die. All of my concentration was on not dying with it. I fought with the controls and time seemed to slow for a few desperate seconds. Thankfully, to my immense relief, I suddenly gained sufficient control to level off. Not before time as the ground loomed up before me. My heart was now racing nineteen to the dozen. The crowd was just ahead, and the show-off in me couldn't help but take the Moth low, buzzing the crowd and making them duck. I laughed to myself as I did it. It worked every time. That was the end of my part of the show.

I landed shortly afterwards, killed the engine and jumped down from the plane. One of the farmhands would gather up the eager members of the crowd so they could have a look at the plane and sit in it. I didn't need to be there for that. I waved at the few people present and bowed while accepting their claps and cheers. In the old days before the war, we really used to draw a crowd, but now … things were different. As I walked towards the old barn that served as a hangar, I stripped off my goggles, hat and gloves. I loosened my long black hair to hang freely about my shoulders. I had always refused to cut it, unlike my sister, even though our mother had suggested it many times.

As I entered the relative shade of the barn, my father Stephen strode up to me. He was wearing his ubiquitous green flat cap and an expression of disapproval.

"Anna," he said without preamble, "what have I told you about pushing the envelope like that?"

"Oh, Daddy, honestly, it wasn't as if I lost control of the plane," I replied.

My sister Jennifer would have formed a far smarter retort. I was always the sensible one, at least according to her.

"And what if you had?" he continued. "What would I tell your mother?"

He always did this, holding the prospect of my mother's grief-stricken countenance over me to tickle my conscience whenever I did something he didn't like. Jennifer would have said something along the lines of, "You'd have to tell her I was dead, wouldn't you?" But then she was made of sterner stuff than me.

"I'm sorry, Daddy. I'll be more careful next time," I replied in my typical conciliatory fashion.

"You girls mean everything to me, darling, and to your mother. You should take more care," he said, smiling and forgiving me at once.

I turned the conversation to something more palatable. "Not much of a crowd today."

He sighed. "No, it's a shame, but it can't be helped."

I touched his arm lightly. "Should we still be doing this? With the war and everything? Shouldn't we be concentrating on the farm?"

Nightingale's Flying Circus may have been a crowd-pleaser in its time, but a part of me felt it wasn't right to continue. My father was a flier, one of the new breed of pilots trained during the Great War. After the war, he'd bought a couple of Tiger Moths and taught Jennifer and I to fly. He'd started up the circus while still running the farm, and he hadn't signed up when war came around again. He and the farm were considered part of an essential industry, keeping food on the table of the nation. Plenty of women were now working the land but, apparently, they needed a man in charge. That always seemed to be the case.

"We're doing our bit," he replied. "We are also entertaining people, giving them something to think about other than the war."

I was still dubious. "Well, if you say so."

"You think too much, Anna, that's your problem," he said with a light laugh.

I gave him a spontaneous hug and he enveloped me in his embrace. Even when he was vexed with me, it was never for very long. There was a discreet cough behind us. We drew apart to see the craggy features of Jim Frazer. He was one of my father's longest-serving farmhands who turned his hand to many things, including being a plane mechanic at times. His face was weatherbeaten, showing his age, and although his back was a little bent from years of hard work, he could still pull his weight around the farm.

"Sorry to disturb you, Governor … Miss," he said. "But there's two gentlemen…"

"Oh," said my father. "I'll come right away."

Jim shot him a deprecating glance. "Pardon, Governor, but it's Miss Anna they've come to see," he said.

"Anna?" said my father.

"Yes, most particular they were, too. City folks, by the looks of it."

"Well, whatever can they want?" my father said testily.

I gave him a look which I hoped might remind him that I was no longer a child. "I'll go and see then, shall I?" I said lightly.

My father nodded as I left the barn. I was brimming with curiosity. Whatever could two gentlemen from the city want with me?

"They're in the library, Miss," Jim called after me. "Clarabelle showed them in there. She thought it were best."

Clarabelle was one of our housemaids. Privileges of being a little well-off as a family, I suppose. I entered the house and went to the bathroom to freshen up before presenting myself to the visitors. I surveyed my complexion in the mirror, adjusting my hair a little. My face was tanned from spending so much time outdoors and flying in an open cockpit. My brown eyes stared back at me critically as I smoothed down my hair. Satisfied enough with my appearance, I made my way to the library.

We lived in a rather large farmhouse. It was a typical Sussex tile-hung two-storey building with plenty of rooms. It had been in the Nightingale family for generations and Jennifer and I had grown up here. My father, too, so I supposed it had been inevitable that he had become a farmer just like his father before him and his grandfather before that.

The house was old with low-beamed ceilings and white walls adorned with pictures. I headed down a long corridor with its fading Persian carpet to arrive at the library. It was one of my favourite places to spend happy hours burrowed in a book when I wasn't flying.

I entered the room and closed the door behind me. Seated in two of the chairs around the unlit fireplace were, indeed, the two gentlemen in question. They were almost identical in appearance, wearing dark suits and white shirts. Both men had black hair and a moustache. The only discernible difference between them, other than that one was wearing a blue tie and the other red, was their eyes. I had excellent eyesight and noticed immediately that one of them possessed grey eyes and the other blue. They were both smoking cigarettes, the smoke from which curled up towards the ceiling.

"Hello," I said. "I'm Anna Nightingale."

The man with the blue eyes took a drag on his cigarette. "Yes," he said. "We know."

"Oh." I was rather taken aback by their insouciant manner. It all seemed rather odd. I began to wonder if I'd done something wrong. Were these policemen? By all appearances, they might be.

"Take a seat, why don't you?" said the one with grey eyes.

It was almost as if they owned the place and it was most disconcerting. However, not wishing to be impolite, I drew up a chair and waited to see what they wanted. They didn't say anything but instead continued to smoke their cigarettes as if they had all the time in the world. It was rather unnerving, to say the least.

"And what are *your* names?" I asked them finally.

"You don't need to know," came the response.

"Oh!" I was surprised at this response; however, I rallied at once. "That could be awkward," I persisted. "I can't just call you … well … *you* … and you won't know which *you* I'm referring to."

"She does have a point," said the one with blue eyes.

"Yes, she does," his colleague agreed.

I began to feel almost as if I had entered the pages of one of my favourite books, *Alice's Adventures in Wonderland*, while they talked about me as if I wasn't even there. I was half expecting a grinning Cheshire cat to appear at any moment.

"You can call us the Marx Brothers," said the man with blue eyes.

"Pardon?" I said, not sure if I had heard him correctly.

"A friend of ours calls us that; he doesn't know we know," said grey eyes. "I'm Harpo and he's Chico."

I was rather incredulous on hearing this explanation. It didn't sound like they were policemen after all. "Really?"

"Those are his nicknames for us," said Harpo with a laugh.

"We rather like it," Chico added.

"A sort of cachet about it," said Harpo. "We'll never tell him, of course."

"Oh, I see," I said, not really seeing at all. So far, I had found the whole interview entirely bizarre. However, since we had got past the introductions, I decided to enquire as to the nature of their business. "So, what brings you here?"

"We're from MI6. Military Intelligence," said Chico.

I experienced a wave of panic and started to mentally review whether I'd done something treasonous recently. "But I'm not a spy," I said at once.

Harpo puffed on his cigarette and regarded me somewhat keenly. "We know you're not," he said. "We're not here about spying."

I was relieved to hear this but naturally even more curious as to the nature of their business. "Then … what?" I asked.

Once again, they took their time in answering. Having finished their cigarettes, they stubbed them out in an ashtray on the coffee table and immediately lit up two more. Chico offered one to me, but I declined. I had never smoked — I didn't like them.

"We're recruiting for something top secret. It involves flying," said Chico at length.

"We need pilots, specifically female pilots, and apparently you're one of the best," said Harpo.

"Well, I wouldn't say *that*," I demurred, not being one to put myself forward.

"You don't need to; we *know* you are," he said, ignoring this remark.

I was nonplussed and still had no idea where the conversation was leading when, without warning, Chico asked, "So … are you in?"

"What? I mean … in what? You haven't told me what it is," I replied.

Harpo shrugged. "We can't tell you unless you're in, and once you're in, you're in," he informed me.

I stared at him.

"It's a conundrum, we know," said Chico sympathetically.

"But … but that's hardly fair. You're asking me to agree to something I don't know anything about," I protested.

Harpo nodded in an understanding way. "The war is not fair, you see, yet here we are fighting it," he said.

"You'll be doing a great service for King and Country," Chico said encouragingly.

"But how?"

"We can't tell you unless you're in," said Chico.

I tried again. "But you want me because I'm a pilot?"

"That's right," said Harpo.

"So, it's something to do with flying?"

Harpo spread his arms apologetically, as if to indicate he could say nothing further.

"Something top secret? To do with the war effort?"

"Bingo," said Chico. "We can't tell you any more than that."

We were no further forward. I sat for a long while in silence. They didn't seem to mind and were content to smoke their cigarettes. My mind was in a whirl. Part of me was immediately tempted by the mystery and intrigue of it all. The other part, the practical part, was pleading for caution, circumspection.

"Can I think about it?" I asked them.

"We will give you two days," said Harpo. "But don't discuss this with anyone … except your sister."

I'd only known these two for a short while, but their capacity to blindside me seemed unlimited. "My sister?"

"Yes, she's already in, you see."

I stared at him in shock. "What?"

"But she can't tell you either. So don't ask her about it," said Chico.

"And this meeting never took place," Harpo added.

The two of them stood up. "We'll see ourselves out," said Harpo.

They moved towards the door as I tried to gather my scattered wits.

"We'll be back in two days," said Chico.

"Toodle pip," said Harpo.

"Wait…" I called after them, but they were gone.

As I sat trying to understand what had just happened, Jennifer bounced into the room. "Have you seen those men?" she said, brim full of excitement. "Isn't it just marvellous?"

I stared at my blonde, blue-eyed sibling while she stood there smiling as if it was Christmas. I loved her to bits but at this moment, I was furious.

"Jenny, how could you?" I said crossly, standing up.

"How could I what?"

"How could you make a decision like that without speaking to me?"

"It's an adventure," she said, pouting just a little. "What's not to like about that? Besides, things are getting boring around here and I want to help with the war effort."

"By doing goodness knows what for goodness knows who?" I said, pacing the room in agitation. "This is just like you, Jenny," I said. "Jumping in feet-first without even thinking about it."

"Oh, Anna, don't be so stuffy," said Jennifer, coming up and taking my hands in hers. "Listen, it's going to be such fun, I'm sure of it. Come on, I don't want to do this without you. I didn't tell you because I thought you'd take it up at once."

"Well then, what is it about?" I asked.

"I can't tell you… It's all top secret … but you'll love it when you do know," she replied, smiling.

"Oh, Jenny, what are you like?" I said with a sigh.

"Won't it be glorious? Doing something heroic," she said, her eyes shining.

"You don't know that, Jenny."

She let go of my hands abruptly. She jutted out her chin in the determined way she had when she'd made up her mind to do something. "Well, I'm going whether you go or not, Anna."

"But you could say you've changed your mind."

"I can't… They said…"

I remembered. She didn't have to tell me. The Marx Brothers had said that once you were in, you were in.

"Anna," said Jennifer, her voice soft. "I will be miserable without you. You know I will."

"That's what you said before you took me apple scrumping at Farmer Jones's orchard," I replied.

"Yes, but wasn't it fun, Anna?"

"Being chased for two miles until Jim saved us…"

Jennifer broke into a peal of laughter. I couldn't help joining her at the recollection.

"Old Jones wasn't happy. He wanted our hides," said Jennifer.

"Thank goodness for Jim."

Jennifer sighed. "You see, you're the sensible one. That's why I need you, and because … because we're a team."

I said no more. I knew that I was fighting a losing battle. There was nothing for it. I came to a decision and threw caution to the wind.

"What is Daddy going to say?" I said at length.

"See! I knew you'd come around."

Jennifer hugged me boisterously. I had serious concerns about the whole thing, but Jennifer had already cast the dice. I reasoned that I had to keep her safe, look after her like a big sister should. The truth was that she was right, too. I wanted an adventure just as much as she did.

CHAPTER TWO

I purposely avoided my father and mother until dinner. I stayed in my room trying to read but to no avail. I thought back to the Marx Brothers. The two of them were somehow compelling. They said a lot without saying anything, and in wartime this was probably exactly how things were done. Top secret things. I had no idea. In that respect, I was somewhat naïve. Not that I wasn't well educated — my parents had seen to that. Jennifer and I had had a string of private tutors to supplement our schooling and I had plenty of books. I'd learned mechanics and practical pursuits too.

At the appointed hour I dressed for dinner. Our father insisted on it. In some ways, he was ridiculously formal for a farmer. Perhaps it harked back to his public-school education and military career.

I joined Jennifer and my parents in the dining room. Clarabelle was in attendance, along with Mary, another housemaid. They were a similar age to me and Jennifer, and we'd grown up with them as they'd taken up their employment from a young age.

I sat down at the table while Clarabelle served me vegetable soup with a freshly baked roll on the side. The advantage of being farmers was that we were better off than most for food. We ate in silence for a while, punctuated by the ticking of the grandfather clock in the corner. My father laid down his spoon.

"Anna, what did those two men want?" he asked.

I hesitated, wondering exactly how to frame my answer, but he took the words out of my mouth.

"You're leaving, aren't you?"

"How did you know?"

He sighed heavily and took a pull from his glass of ale. "I'm not daft, Anna. I can recognise men from the Ministry when I see them. You're a pilot and… I always thought they would come looking for you and your sister one day."

"What?"

My mother Catherine entered the conversation. "What your father means is that we know they are looking for pilots, women pilots to fly planes, deliver them and so forth. We've discussed it."

I knew that too, but what the Marx Brothers wanted didn't sound anything like that. I glanced at Jennifer, but her expression gave nothing away.

"Yes, yes, of course," I said. "But you never mentioned your discussions to me, either of you, or the business about them wanting pilots to transport planes."

It just showed how much I hadn't been paying attention to current affairs. I had tried to keep the war at arm's length, and now the war had come to me.

"We … we were reluctant to lose you … either of you," my mother replied.

"It's my fault," said my father. "I wanted to continue the circus somehow, keep you girls around, but that's probably selfish of me, I know."

"No, Daddy, it's not," said Jennifer. "But we have to do our duty."

"Of course," he said.

"When are you going?" my mother asked.

"I don't know," I said, looking at Jennifer. "They are coming back in two days. I haven't said yes to them yet, but Jenny has and I think we should stick together."

"Well, naturally you must say yes," said my father. "It's the right thing to do." He grunted, satisfied, and signalled to Clarabelle to clear the plates.

The die was cast. I hadn't expected our father to be so easily in favour of it. Then again, he didn't really know what we were signing up for, and neither did we.

The Marx Brothers had returned, as promised, two days later, and informed me they were delighted I had accepted. They then proceeded to tell me nothing further but instead provided Jennifer and me with papers and directions to Hawberry Hall, which was to the northeast of Cambridge. Three days later, we departed.

The Hall was set deep in the countryside and we entered by a large gate which was guarded very assiduously by sentries. Prominently displayed notices proclaimed it to be the property of the Ministry of Defence. From the car windows, I could see that the boundary of the land was well-fenced and walled off.

Jennifer and I had driven ourselves there. Our father had given us the use of one of the family cars. It was a small MG Roadster two-seater with a soft top cover. It had just enough room for our bags but nothing else. It had been something of a tearful goodbye. I had never left our home for long, and now I didn't know when we'd be back.

The sentry on duty scrutinised our papers thoroughly before allowing us through the gate. That being done, I let out the clutch and we proceeded up a long driveway lined with trees until we finally pulled up in front of the Hall itself.

"Well, would you look at that!" said Jennifer in disbelief.

"It's…"

"Absolutely bloody massive," she finished for me. She got out of the car and stood admiring what was apparently to be our new home.

Hawberry Hall was impressive. At least three storeys high, it was what might be termed 'a pile' by the aristocracy. The building sprawled out in front of us, stretching either side and seemingly endless at first glance. It was set in flat, well-kept grounds. I had parked the car on the gravel outside the front. There were a few cars already parked there, as well as a couple of trucks and army vehicles.

"Come on, Anna," said Jennifer. "Let's go inside."

There didn't seem to be anyone about. We got our bags from the back of the car and climbed a wide set of stone stairs towards the imposing portico. It sported fluted columns. The entire building appeared to be constructed from pale stone, punctuated by large windows.

We entered through the open front door to find ourselves in an atrium of sorts. It rose above us to a glass-panelled roof. There was a staircase in the centre going up to the first floor and panelled walls with doors leading to what could be rooms, or even corridors. In the centre of the atrium sat a desk at which resided a woman in uniform. The desk had several telephones, a typewriter, and various writing implements, as one might expect. I assumed this must be the reception.

We approached and the woman looked up at us and smiled.

"Ah, newcomers, I take it," she said.

"Yes, that's right. I'm Anna Nightingale and this is Jennifer, my sister."

She consulted a list on a clipboard for a moment, made a couple of ticks and then stood up. "I'm Sergeant Martha Pryde," she said, holding out her hand. "Welcome to Hawberry Hall."

"Thank you," I said, shaking her hand in return.

"I'll show you to your quarters," she said. "The others should all arrive soon, and there will be a general briefing tomorrow morning after breakfast. I assume you two don't mind sharing?"

I glanced at Jennifer. She smiled. "No, of course not."

"All right then, follow me."

We walked up the staircase and along what seemed to be endless corridors. It was certainly a vast mansion and I wondered who it had belonged to. The walls held a plethora of paintings, some of which probably depicted the previous incumbents. Martha didn't say much, and we glanced about us curiously until we arrived at what was apparently the door to our room.

"In here," Martha said. "Make yourselves at home. You are lucky — this room has a bathroom. We've also got central heating, thank goodness. Dinner will be served at six when you hear the gong. Come down to the main entrance where you came in and someone will show you where to go from there." She opened the door and stepped aside to let us in. "Is there anything else you need right now?"

"Should we let Daddy know we've arrived?" Jennifer asked me.

"There's a telephone you can use if you need to," said Martha. "Just let me know and I'll show you where it is."

"Thank you," I said. "Jenny, we can call them later."

Martha smiled.

"We've never really been away from home," I told her.

"It's quite all right," she said. "I understand. Takes a bit of getting used to."

She walked away smartly. Her footsteps echoed down the empty corridor.

"Look at this," said Jennifer, walking into our new abode. "Isn't it marvellous?"

I turned my attention to the room. It was large and well furnished with a double bed, one single bed against the wall, wardrobes, and a dressing table. The style of the entire house was Georgian with ornate plaster mouldings on the ceiling. The wallpaper was a pleasant shade of green with a fleur-de-lis pattern in gold. Large windows revealed the formal gardens at the back of the house, which stretched away into woodland.

"It is very nice," I agreed, examining the bathroom.

"I'll say," said Jennifer. "Such high ceilings. I'll feel like Lady Muck here."

We laughed. It was certainly grander than our home, and I had thought that quite grand.

"Come on, Jenny, let's unpack."

We stayed up in our room for a while, feeling initially rather shy about exploring the house in case there were places we weren't supposed to go. However, curiosity got the better of us both and as it was going on for dinner time shortly, we decided to see what we could discover.

"It's awfully quiet, isn't it?" said Jennifer as we wandered up and down several empty corridors. "Do you think we're the only ones here?"

Just then we passed an open door, beyond which seemed to be a sitting room of sorts. I didn't want to be too inquisitive and intrude but Jennifer had other ideas.

"What's in here?" she said, walking right in as if she owned the place.

"Jenny!" I hissed, but it was too late; I felt obliged to follow her.

To my acute embarrassment, I saw there was a man sitting behind a desk at one end of the room. He looked to be around thirty-five years of age, with black hair and a moustache. He had a kindly, rather handsome face and brown eyes. He stood up when we came in. I noticed he was wearing uniform.

"Can I help you?" he said, coming forward to meet us.

"Sorry … we're new here," I said, feeling myself blushing furiously. "We were just looking around."

"You must be two of the recruits," he said, smiling. "Wing Commander James Donnington at your service." He held out his hand.

"Anna Nightingale," I said as I shook it. "And this is my sister, Jennifer."

"Pleased to have you aboard," he said.

Just then the sound of a gong reverberated through the still air.

"Ah," said James. "Sounds like dinner."

"Oh gosh," I said. "Shouldn't we change … or something?"

"No need," James told me. "Come as you are. You'll soon be wearing uniform anyway. I'll show you the way."

Dinner was served in a large room supplied with several tables. The ceiling was even more ornate, with cherubs painted in the Renaissance style and burnished with gold leaf. There were a large number of women in civvies, plus other uniformed personnel, all of whom had appeared as if from nowhere. There was a buffet-style table at one end, with people serving food from large aluminium receptacles kept warm using candles underneath. We hesitated in the entrance to the dining room.

"Go and get yourselves some grub," suggested James. "Sit anywhere you like. Get to know the other recruits."

With that, he left us to join some of his fellow officers.

"Come on," said Jennifer. "Might as well get stuck in."

We stood in line and received a plate of stew each with mash and cabbage. There was apple pie and custard for dessert. Water was provided at the tables. We chose an empty table and sat down.

"At least the food's good," said Jennifer, tucking in.

I could certainly agree. I had just taken a forkful when we were joined by four other women.

"Hello, pleased to meet you," said one of them, setting down her tray. "I'm Maria Preston. Are you here for the secret squirrel business?"

She had blonde hair and blue eyes, and her voice had a Welsh lilt to it.

"Yes, we are," said Jennifer.

"This is Shelly Cartwright, Connie Broadbent and Patricia Batley," Maria continued, indicating her companions in turn. "Shelly and I are from the same hometown."

I wondered if they had all been recruited in the same way we had. No doubt we'd find out in time. For the moment we satisfied ourselves with small talk. Shelly, also blonde, turned out to be Welsh too, while redhaired Connie was from Leeds and Patricia from Manchester.

The dining room became a hubbub of noise which was rather overwhelming. Jennifer seemed to be in her element and was soon discussing the merits of the Tiger Moth with Connie, who was apparently an aircraft mechanic. When she'd finished eating, Connie lit up a cigarette and offered them around. Jennifer took one and shot me a sly smile.

When the meal came to an end, James stood up and called for silence.

"Welcome, everyone," he said. "We are now going to repair to the briefing room."

Those who I assumed to be recruits were filing out of the dining room and so we followed.

"Doesn't this feel rather like the first day at school?" said Shelly with a grin.

We walked into another rather ornate room with a raised section at the end. There was a large map of Europe on the wall and chairs set out in rows.

"Don't sit at the front," hissed Shelly.

"Oh, you never change," said Maria, laughing.

We took seats near the back and settled down to wait for whatever was going to transpire. Eventually, James appeared and stood up on the podium. With him were two people I recognised: the Marx Brothers. There was also a woman in uniform standing beside them. The room fell silent.

"Welcome," James said. "For those I haven't yet met, I'm Wing Commander James Donnington. I am in charge of what will be your unit. We were going to hold this briefing in the morning but since everyone has arrived, we elected to bring it forward. Time is of the essence, as they say." He paused for a moment. "Beside me is Wing Officer Gloria Shepherd, who is my second-in-command. The two gentlemen are our colleagues from MI6."

I wondered if he knew about their nicknames but if he did, he didn't say anything. I turned my attention back to what James was saying.

"You're here because you have been selected for your skills. You've been invited, in fact, to become part of a top-secret initiative, an elite unit made up almost entirely of women. The missions you will be asked to undertake will all involve flying. You will be asked to sign the Official Secrets Act and from that point forward sworn to secrecy. Your actions will remain a secret for the duration of the war and probably beyond it."

Nobody spoke and all eyes were on James.

"The missions will be dangerous, and I would be remiss in my duty if I didn't tell you there's a chance that some of you may not survive; but make no mistake, your work will be vital to the war effort. Accordingly, I'm giving you all a chance to back out. If you wish to do so, raise your hand now and you will be processed out of the facility."

He waited, but no hands were raised. Jennifer glanced at me, her eyes shining with excitement. This was still a lark to her. For me, it was becoming all too real. But there was no way I would leave my sister to do this on her own, regardless of any misgivings I might have.

"As I can see, you're all keen to fly in the face of danger," James said. "I'm happy therefore to get started. You will all be inducted into the unit and this will mean passing a medical. You will sign the Official Secrets Act, as I said, as well as the papers which will make you part of the RAF, or rather the WAAF. You will be issued with a rank and a uniform. Any questions?"

There were none, and we were duly dismissed. The next few hours were a whirlwind. We were sent from pillar to post signing documents, undergoing physical examinations and filling in forms. Finally, we were each issued with a uniform and I proudly put it on.

"Well, Section Officer Nightingale," I said to Jennifer when were back in our room. "How do I look?"

"You look marvellous, Section Officer Nightingale," she said. "What about me?"

"Splendid."

She came up to me and gave me a spontaneous hug. "Can you believe it?" she said. "We're going to be pilots in the RAF!"

"The WAAF," I corrected her. "The Women's Auxiliary Air Force."

"Oh, same difference. We're in the Air Force!"

"I wonder what we're going to be doing, though. James said it would be dangerous," I mused.

"Yes... Isn't it exciting?"

I wouldn't have called the prospect of being killed exciting, but I didn't want to dampen my sister's enthusiasm. "Yes, Jenny, of course it is, darling. Anyway, let's get some sleep. Save that excitement for tomorrow, hmm?"

"You sound just like Mummy," she laughed.

I remembered with a guilty pang that we hadn't yet phoned our parents. It would have to wait until we got a chance the next day.

We lay together in the double bed, just like when we were children. Neither of us wanted to be alone in the single bed. It felt strange leaving home so abruptly, for a new life with so many unknowns. We would find out soon enough what we'd let ourselves in for. We had signed our service contracts and there was no turning back. I closed my eyes on that thought and went to sleep.

CHAPTER THREE

Breakfast was a boisterous affair. Porridge, eggs on toast, fried spam and baked beans were the order of the day. Cups of tea and coffee were available from large tureens. We joined Maria and the others at what would probably become our usual table. It turned out that their rooms were not far from ours in the same corridor. We were all full of anticipation for the briefing to come. Our purpose here would finally be divulged.

"Well, I reckon we're going after Hitler," said Shelly, consuming her breakfast with relish.

"Oh stop!" said Maria. "Don't mind her, she's full of such nonsense from reading too many trashy spy novels."

"They're not trashy," Shelly objected.

"What do you think this is really all about?" said Connie, ignoring Shelly's somewhat far-fetched notion.

"Your guess is as good as mine," said Patricia.

We fell silent. I looked at their respective ranks. Connie, Maria and Shelly were all Assistant Section Officers and Patricia was a Section Officer. I wondered what it all meant. The conversation moved on to other topics and I let it all wash over me as I concentrated on my breakfast. I still wasn't used to the hustle and bustle.

Connie lit up a cigarette and shared it with Jennifer. I supposed I would have to get used to her smoking more regularly.

With breakfast over, we repaired to the briefing room. Just as we had got seated, Gloria walked in and barked out, "Attention!" in a very loud voice.

We looked at each other, not sure what to do.

"I know none of you have had any drill practice," said Gloria, "but now you are in uniform, you stand to attention when a senior officer comes into the room. Like this." She stood smartly to attention.

We all stood up and tried to follow suit.

"You'll be getting some drill practice, don't you worry," she said with a smile and made her way to the podium.

We remained standing as James walked in and nodded at us in approval. He was followed by the Marx Brothers. They took their places on the podium.

"Stand easy," said James. "You may all sit down."

We did so and I exchanged glances with the others.

"It is like being back at school," Shelly whispered.

Maria quickly hushed her.

James cleared his throat. "Now you're all signed up," he began, "I can officially welcome you to the Sirens."

There must have been some puzzled looks on faces at this announcement.

"Let me tell you a story," he continued. "It's a story about someone who believed that perhaps women might have a combat role in this war. History bears this out. You've probably heard of the Amazons? Cleopatra, Joan of Arc, Boudicca? All formidable female warriors. In mythology too there was Diana, the Roman goddess who was a fearsome hunter. And the Sirens, who lured sailors to their destruction in dangerous waters with their song."

He paused. He had certainly gained everyone's attention.

"This person spent a considerable amount of time arguing the case for a specialised unit. A secret strike force that could damage the enemy in places where it counts. The argument met refusal after refusal … until…"

His voice dropped a little in the silent room.

"Until it dawned on certain members of the upper echelons of command that we were running out of men. Pilots, to be specific — we didn't have enough to go around. And that is when I struck … because the person I'm talking about was none other than myself."

There was an air of expectancy in the room.

"I've been told many things," James continued. "That women are not up to the job. Too emotional. Unable to do what a man can do. Yes, I've heard it all. And I don't believe any of it. And *you* are going to prove them wrong."

I glanced at Jennifer. I had not seen her look quite so excited since the first time she was allowed to fly solo in the Tiger Moth.

"The Sirens," James said, "is the name of a squadron, *this* squadron, and it will be as deadly as those myths foretold. You are all now members of an elite strike force which will carry out missions against enemy targets in Europe. You will be flying the de Havilland Mosquito, a superlative aircraft. Some of you will be pilots and some of you will be navigators, working together as a two-woman team. Pilots have been given the rank of Section Officer and navigators Assistant Section Officer. There will be ample opportunity for promotion as time goes on. Your training will begin today. You will learn things like drill and, of course, flying — not only the Mosquito but some of the other aircraft we have here too. In due course, you will fly your first mission. Do you have any questions?"

A hand went up at the front.

"Yes, Section Officer Harris?"

"I was just wondering, what do we tell our friends and family?"

"You tell them you're transporting planes," said James.

"But isn't that the job of the Air Transport Auxiliary?" asked Section Officer Harris. "I'm asking because I was in the ATA and now I'm in the Air Force; won't they wonder at it?"

"Consider it a promotion," James said with a smile. "The ATA do a fantastic job, of course, but nobody in the RAF was going to give command of this unit to any other branch of the services."

There was a ripple of laughter at this.

"So, you can say you're helping out the ATA — flying planes, training pilots and so on. Just leave it at that. In fact, there's no need to tell anyone anything unless you have to."

"The less you say," interjected Harpo, "the fewer questions people will be inclined to ask."

"People make their own explanations," added Chico. "In the end, it doesn't matter what they think. What matters is that they don't know the truth about this unit."

"Exactly," said James. "Does that answer your question?"

"Yes, sir, thank you, sir," said Section Officer Harris.

"Any other questions?" said James affably. "Yes, Assistant Section Officer Baker?"

"How long before we fly our first mission?" asked a young woman who sounded Welsh.

"I was coming to that," said James. "It will be a few weeks yet. There is a lot to learn in a short space of time. Be prepared for some intensive training."

Another hand went up.

"You said these will be two-woman teams. Who gets to choose the teams?"

"You will make your choices in due course," said James. "We prefer bonds to form naturally due to the close-knit nature of a Mosquito flying team. You have to work almost as one symbiotic unit. So, we feel it's better if you find the navigator or pilot you think you can best work with. You will be asked to choose in due course, but I'm sure many of you will have decided far sooner than that."

Harpo spoke again. "These missions are of vital importance. I cannot stress that enough. You need to have absolute trust in all the members of your squadron. Remember that you have one another's back. We want you all to return in one piece from these missions."

"And if we don't?" asked Shelly.

"I'll put it to you like this," said Chico. "These are life or death missions. There is no in-between."

The import of what he'd just told us dawned on me and no doubt several others, judging by their expressions.

"There will be plenty of time to ask all the questions you want during training," said James. "I'll hand over to Wing Officer Shepherd, to get things underway."

The CO briefly nodded to Gloria and then left the stage.

"Since there are so many of you, you will be divided into four groups of six," said Gloria. "There will be two pilot groups and two navigator groups. There will be different training sessions for pilots and navigators. It goes without saying that everyone will be doing drill."

There was a collective groan and Gloria laughed good-naturedly. "Consider yourselves lucky you haven't had to do basic training," she said. "There are some advantages to being part of the Sirens. You need to know just enough protocol in case the top brass appear on the base. There will be four sets of sessions per day, two in the morning, two in the afternoon, with breaks in between and a break for lunch. If anyone becomes sick or injured, they must report it immediately. We have on-site medical facilities. Consider this briefing room your HQ for the moment. Any questions?"

Nobody raised their hand, so Gloria continued. "On the noticeboard at the back of the room, you'll find the list of your assigned groups. You will also find the timetable of classes, where you are supposed to be and when."

A hand shot up. "Yes?" said Gloria. "ASO Jones, is it?"

I noticed she had shortened the rank to an acronym.

"What about socialising?" asked Cynthia Jones in a broad Scottish brogue.

"Are you tired of us already?" Gloria quipped.

There was some laughter at this.

"No, I just wonder if there's some place a woman can get a drink?"

Gloria took the question equally enough. "We have our own in-house bar, in case you hadn't discovered it already. And there's a billiard room, gymnasium, and even an outdoor pool if you're brave enough. We've all the facilities here, a library, games, and so forth."

"Oh, aye, thanks … but what about leaving the base?" said Cynthia.

"You can leave the base if you wish to go further afield, but if it's for an overnight stay or leave, then you will require a pass. Think of Hawberry Hill almost as a ship on the ocean and you won't go too far wrong."

It was obvious that leaving the base was to be discouraged. I could see why. We were no ordinary unit. We were something special and as such we'd better start behaving that way from the off. We weren't the only personnel on the base in any case. There were support staff, training staff, mechanics and more. A whole raft of personnel, in fact, to support the Sirens. The missions we were going to fly must be incredibly important to warrant it.

"Thank you, ma'am," said Cynthia.

"Right, let's get to it," Gloria said. "Find your groups and then get to your classes."

As one, we all went to the back of the room and crowded around the noticeboard. I had been put in Group Athena along with Jennifer, Patricia, SO Carol Davies, SO Susan Bell and SO Virginia Goodman. The other three groups were named Demeter, Hera and Calliope. I had read enough classics to know these were named after Greek goddesses. I wondered if these were James's choices.

"I'm glad we're together," said Jennifer, giving me a hug.

"So am I," I replied.

And so, it began.

CHAPTER FOUR

The days flew by, turning into weeks before we knew it. We went back to basics at flight school, learning the theory that I probably should have known but my father had never taught me. We studied evasion techniques and combat in the air. Pilots needed to know the rudiments of navigation, while the navigators underwent an intensive course. We would rely on them totally during a mission and their skills needed to be up to the mark.

Then there was drill. Our instructor was Sergeant Frances Wallace. She was something of a tartar from the off. Marching up and down with rifles was not our favourite occupation; however, we gradually began to feel like a cohesive unit.

Finally, the day came when we would be allowed to fly. We had assembled in the briefing room to get our orders. James and Gloria entered the room to an expectant hush.

"I've heard great things about all of you from your instructors," James said. "It vindicates everything that those of us who believe in this squadron have fought for, so well done."

I couldn't help but smile at this. I had tried my best and I knew the others had too. We had a reputation to build.

"Today is the day I'm sure you've all been waiting for. You're finally going to get up in the air. Take it easy and enjoy it."

There were a few cheers while Gloria took over.

"Everyone to the front of the building, where the trucks will take you to the airfield," she ordered. We hadn't yet seen the airfield.

We filed out in a buzz of excitement. We had each been issued with a pale brown flying suit and a sheepskin jacket, along with leather flying boots. Each of us was wearing a lifejacket and a sheepskin flying helmet. Our parachutes were kept in the plane. Mine would be on the pilot's seat and the navigator's tucked in front of them. We had sat in a cut-down, simulated version of the Mosquito cockpit many times so that we were familiar with the controls. Now was our chance to actually fly one. I had paired up with Maria, who would be flying as my navigator. Jennifer had taken a shine to Shelly. They were similar in disposition, so it was a good match.

The trucks wended their way down a tarmac road at the side of Hawberry Hall which, after a short drive through the woods, opened out onto a wide stretch of land. It was, to our surprise, the airfield, barely a mile or so from the Hall. There were large hangars painted in camouflage. On the grass on one side sat a line of twelve Mosquitos, and some other assorted aircraft. It was one of those twelve I would be flying in.

We climbed aboard and took off.

"I was starting to think we'd never get to fly one of these," I said to Maria as I opened up the throttle on the Mosquito for the first time. The Rolls-Royce engines responded with a purr as we were kicked back into our seats and raced up the runway.

"Wow, this is amazing," said Maria as the wheels left the ground.

This was nothing like a Tiger Moth. This was flying a dream, a beautiful twin-engined aircraft built out of wood.

"Just take it easy, Bluebird One, and bring it back in one piece."

It was Flight Lieutenant Henry Peterson, our flying instructor, over the radio. Bluebird was the codename we were currently using when flying. We were told these would be different on an actual mission. He was observing us from the air, flying in a Spitfire.

"Wilco," I replied. "Now then, let's see what this girl can do," I said quietly to Maria. I opened up the throttle.

The Mosquito could hit a top speed in excess of four hundred miles an hour, which Henry had assured us could outrun the current German fighters on the flat. It was a comforting thought, although a German fighter was the last thing I would expect to see in Cambridgeshire.

I took the Mosquito through its paces, gaining confidence with every turn. It was exhilarating. We were flying the Mosquito fighter-bomber variant equipped with four Hispano cannons and four Browning machine guns. I wondered if they were loaded. Nobody had said, and gunnery practice wasn't on the cards today. I parked the thought and put my attention back on the plane.

"That's enough, Bluebirds. Bring it in," said Henry at last. It seemed only a moment since we'd taken off, but our watches showed we'd been flying for at least thirty minutes.

We'd had our fun, wheeling, banking and diving around the airfield and its environs, keeping a sharp eye out for each other. A collision was the last thing we needed. Fortunately, there had been no near-misses. However, we'd not started formation flying yet, or low-level flying, which would be far more dangerous and taxing.

As we manoeuvred into position for the final approach, Maria said urgently, "What's that over there?"

I flicked a glance over to the left where she was pointing. It was a plane.

"Is that what I think it is?" I replied, trying to recall my aircraft recognition.

"It's a Focke-Wulf," said Maria. "Oh my God, what do we do?"

The German fighter plane was heading towards our squadron, closing in at speed. What was it we were supposed to say? Then I remembered. "Bandit, bandit at nine o'clock, coming in fast," I said urgently over the radio.

Henry responded at once. "Abort landing, Bluebirds, and break, split up. Do not engage; leave this to me."

I banked away rapidly as we'd been told to do. Henry turned his Spitfire towards the enemy plane. Where *had* it come from? There wasn't time to think about it.

The German continued on an inexorable course. Even though our planes were dispersing, I could tell he was making a beeline for one of them. I knew exactly who it was. My heart sank.

"Jenny," I said to Maria. "He's going after Jenny."

"Don't worry," said Maria. "Henry's going to stop him."

I could see that Henry's Spitfire was indeed on an intercept with the Wulf.

"Bluebird Four," I said frantically to Jennifer. "Watch out!"

"I've seen him," said Jennifer, turning her plane away and opening up the throttle.

My thoughts raced. What if Henry didn't get the Wulf? What if Jennifer couldn't get away fast enough? Without a second thought, I opened up the throttle and set a course for the Jerry plane. I'd looked out for my sister all my life, and I wasn't going to stop now.

"Anna, what are you doing?" said Maria in alarm.

I had already decided on my course of action. "Finding out if there's any ammo in these guns," I told her grimly, slipping off the safety catch. I tried to remember what I'd been taught about firing the guns. Line up the target in the gunsight, then fire the cannons or the Brownings.

"Anna…" said Maria again, but it was too late.

Instinct took over. The Wulf was in my sights and I fired a burst from the cannons. I had been told these were the deadlier weapon. Simultaneously, Henry opened fire from the German's flank.

At least one of us hit the enemy plane, and the Wulf exploded into a fireball. Shards of metal flew in our direction as I pulled a tight turn. We narrowly avoided being hit as I throttled us away from danger.

"Holy moly, that was close," said Maria.

"Damn right," I said with relief.

"Bluebirds, resume landing. The threat has been eliminated," said Henry over the radio.

"Roger," came the response from twelve aircraft as we lined up our approach once more.

One by one we landed and taxied to our designated standings. I applied the brakes and the Mosquito came to a stop.

The excitement over, it dawned on us both that there would probably be consequences.

"What do you think is going to happen?" asked Maria, referring to my shooting down the Wulf.

"I don't know," I told her, "but it was my decision, and if there's any flak to be taken then I'll take it. I'm used to it anyway. My father has told me off for wayward behaviour more times than I can count."

Maria laughed and the tension between us eased. "No," she said. "We're a team. If we get into trouble, then we do it together."

I killed the engines and reached over to squeeze her hand. "Thanks," I said.

"That's why I picked you," said Maria after a moment. "For my pilot."

"Why?" I asked her curiously.

"Because I sensed you would do the right thing in a crisis."

"Well, maybe I picked you too," I said, smiling.

We left the Mosquito through the side door and jumped down to the ground. There was a thin telescopic ladder which we could use to climb in and out, but jumping down seemed easier.

Before I could do anything, Jennifer came running up and gave me a hug.

"I saw what you did," she said. "Thank you for trying to save me."

"That was pretty good shooting, missus," said Shelly.

"Uh oh, here comes trouble," said Maria under her breath.

Henry was walking towards us. His expression was unreadable.

We snapped to attention and saluted. He returned the salute perfunctorily.

"At ease," he said, turning his attention to me. "Rather a good thing I thought to have the weapons loaded, don't you think, Anna?"

"Yes, sir," I replied.

"We'll discuss the ramifications later," he said. "Good shooting, though." With that, he turned on his heel and left.

"Sounds ominous," said Shelly.

I nodded. The last thing I needed was to end up on the carpet the first time I got to fly.

"Well, I think it was jolly good of you," said Jennifer loyally.

"Thanks, Jenny. I can always rely on you."

"Come on, let's get back to Hawberry and face the music," said Maria.

Arm in arm, we headed over to the trucks.

Over lunch in the dining room, several of the others came up to congratulate me on shooting down the Wulf.

"That was damn good shooting," said Patricia.

"I'm not sure Henry thinks so," I replied.

"Oh stuff, we think so and that's what counts," she countered.

I wasn't quite so confident. Maria shot me a reassuring smile. The food went some way to restoring my good humour. It was game pie, with mash, vegetables and gravy, followed by a sponge pudding with custard. By the time Flight Sergeant Judy Royston appeared in front of me, I was feeling more the thing. Her arrival was expected. Judy was James's adjutant. She was a petite brunette with curly brown hair, eyes to match and a rose complexion.

"The CO would like to see you in his office, ma'am," she said.

I exchanged glances with the others at the table and stood up.

"I'm coming too," said Maria, getting out of her chair.

I was glad to have Maria at my back. We accompanied Judy up the stairs and along various corridors to the familiar sitting-room-cum-office where James resided. She stood aside to let us enter and then left. In the room were James, Gloria and Henry, all seated around a table.

"You've brought a delegation, I see," said James with a smile.

"We're a team, sir," said Maria. "Where Anna goes, I go."

"Spoken like a trooper," James observed. "Very well, take a seat, both of you."

We sat down at the table and waited.

"What were you thinking, Anna," said James conversationally after a few moments, "when you decided to engage the Focke-Wulf?"

I hesitated, gathering my thoughts. "My first thought was to protect my sister, sir. The German was heading straight for her," I said.

"Didn't Flight Lieutenant Peterson tell you not to engage?"

"He did, sir, but I evaluated the chances of him eliminating the threat and decided that perhaps he could use some help."

This surprised a crack of laughter from the three of them.

"You know Henry is a Battle of Britain Fighter Ace, don't you?" said James, sounding amused.

"I am aware of that, sir, but nevertheless two shots are often better than one … to perhaps tip the odds in our favour."

"So, this was a purely altruistic gesture on your part, to protect your sister?"

"Sir, I protect my own. My sister is my own, as is every member of this squadron, sir. They are all my sisters now, and I will do my damnedest to protect them. It's not altruism, it's family," I said passionately.

"I second that," said Maria, suddenly finding her voice. "And I damn well agree with it. What Anna did was bloody marvellous! And if you're going to tell her off for doing it, then you can tell me off too…"

She clapped a hand to her mouth at this and shot me a guilty look.

"This spirit," James said easily, "is exactly what I was hoping for."

"Really?" I said, surprised.

"Yes, really. It's the attitude that breeds a successful mission. Thinking on your feet and taking the odd risk, when necessary, regardless of the consequences. You didn't know whether the guns were loaded, but you went for it anyway. That's what I want from my Sirens: initiative. You've shown me that you have what it takes."

I stared at him, flabbergasted. I had expected a dressing down, and instead here he was complimenting me on what I'd done.

"Don't look so shocked," he said, seeing my expression. "Obeying orders is one thing, but it isn't always the right thing. In this case, you did the right thing."

"Don't think that's carte blanche to disobey orders, though," Henry put in.

"No, sir."

"I'm making you Flight Leader," said James. "That means you will fly the lead aircraft on the missions."

He could have knocked me down with a feather. All I could do was stare at him.

"Any questions?" he continued, smiling at my discomposure.

"No, sir."

"Keep it up and there'll be a promotion in it for you."

"Yes, sir, thank you, sir."

"Dismissed."

I left the office a little stunned. When we were out of earshot, Maria let out a whoop. "Did you hear that? Flight bloody Leader, no less. Well done, Anna! Bloody well deserved."

"I hope you're right," I replied, feeling a little overwhelmed.

"You'll be fine," she said, tucking her arm in mine. "You'll see."

The others were all agog to hear what had transpired, but I wasn't able to tell them because a briefing had been called almost as soon as we arrived back in the dining room.

"Attention!" said Gloria loudly.

We all sprang to our feet as James, Gloria, Henry and the Marx Brothers took to the podium.

"At ease, sit down," said James with his usual equanimity. "I just want to go over what happened at flight practice."

He paused and I felt as if he was looking straight at me for a moment. I experienced something of a flutter under his gaze but quickly quelled it. In any case, he had resumed talking.

"First of all, the appearance of that Focke-Wulf was, we believe, purely coincidental. We've no reason to believe Jerry has any idea about our operation and we aim to keep it that way. My MI6 colleagues assure me that's the case."

"That is correct," added Harpo. "We checked with our various contacts and there is nothing to suggest that the Germans know anything about the Sirens. Continued secrecy is therefore imperative."

"Precisely so," said James. "Anyway, we will move on from that to the actions of SO Anna Nightingale."

He paused and there were a number of glances in my direction.

"Ordinarily, we don't condone disobeying orders," he said. "However, in this case, Anna evaluated a threat and acted. Quick thinking, smart thinking, appropriate action, that's what counts in battle. That's what we saw today. Anna took a risk, and it paid off. Accordingly, she will now be your Flight Leader."

There was a spontaneous cheer which I thought began with Shelly.

"Now that you've had a go in the Mosquitos," James continued, "you'll be learning to fly in formation, navigating for real, strafing and bombing practice, low-level flying and more. We need you mission fit as soon as possible."

It sounded to me as if there was something in offing. No doubt we would discover was it was soon enough.

"That will be all. Dismissed," said James.

Later that evening Jennifer and I sat together with Maria, Shelly, Patricia and Connie in our room. Shelly had somehow obtained a bottle of gin and we sat on the bed, passing it between us. Connie and Jennifer were near the window, sharing a cigarette, which seemed to have become their thing.

"Where did you get this?" Maria asked Shelly.

"Now that would be telling," said Shelly.

"As long as you didn't nick it," her friend admonished her.

"Of course I didn't nick it. It's just a favour for a favour…"

"Oh God, don't tell me. I don't want to know," said Maria.

We all laughed. Shelly made a face.

"I just promised the barman I'd go on a date with him, that's all. Anyway," Shelly continued, "what do you think of James? He's rather a dish, don't you think?"

Maria passed me the bottle and I took a swig of gin, grimacing slightly.

"Don't you go setting your cap at him," Maria told Shelly. "He's our commanding officer."

"A girl can look," said Shelly with a smirk.

As I listened to them, my mind drifted. I wasn't ready to be interested in men — one reason being the fact I'd split up from my boyfriend, Nigel Braithwaite, just before we'd left for Hawberry.

The conversation hadn't gone particularly well.

"I'm going away," I had said to Nigel once Jennifer and I had told the Marx Brothers our decision.

We were sitting on a fallen log on the edge of one of the big fields which opened out to a view beyond. His head jerked up at this pronouncement.

"To do what?"

"It's for the war, but I can't tell you…" I said.

"What about us? I thought we'd get married … spend our life together…" He trailed off, seeing my expression.

We'd never discussed the future before and I was surprised.

"Perhaps you just presumed," I said.

"Well … I did … of course… Our parents…"

I cut him short. "You assumed too much. You didn't even ask me what I thought about it."

"Well, I'm asking now!" he said, beginning to get annoyed.

"I'm sorry, Nigel. This is something I have to do. I don't know how long I am going to be gone for, and it wouldn't be fair to ask you to wait," I said, trying to soften it.

He was silent, looking at me with eyes now full of resentment. "You don't love me … do you?" he said at length.

I couldn't bring myself to say it, although what he said was true. I just hadn't wanted to face it before.

"It doesn't matter, I can see it in your face. Well, enjoy your … whatever it is you're going to do…"

He turned and walked away. This wasn't how I had meant the conversation to go. I hadn't wanted to end things so abruptly. I felt bad for him and called after him, but he didn't turn around. I watched him getting smaller in the distance. The most prominent emotion I felt then was relief.

"Anna…"

It was Jennifer. She touched my arm. I opened my eyes and realised I had dozed off.

"Where are the others?" I said, noting the empty bed.

"They left. We could see you were tired."

"I was thinking of Nigel," I told her.

"Don't fret. It's over and done with," she replied sympathetically.

"That's just it… I'm not fretting."

CHAPTER FIVE

There was no more time to think about Nigel or romance in the ensuing days. Now we were flying, it was nonstop exercises. We began with formation flying. I was now Bluebird Leader, out in front of the formation and directing the flight. It was nerve-racking, but since James had put his faith in me, I was determined to do my best.

Formation flying was followed by point-to-point navigation. We carried out strafing and bombing practice runs, then finally low-level flying. We were briefed by Henry.

"Today we're going to fly low level, and when I say low level, I mean as low as you can go: skimming hedges and treetops. We're sticking to a route which has very few houses for obvious reasons. The lead navigator will follow the route exactly as it's mapped out."

I glanced at Maria, who didn't look in the least nervous. She was turning into a first-class navigator. I relied on her implicitly.

"Make no mistake," said Henry, "this is very dangerous. It's not to be taken lightly. You must be alert to hazards like telegraph lines and water towers. If you hit something at the speed you'll be flying, then I don't fancy your chances. You won't be high enough to bail out."

I looked at Jennifer and she looked at me. Things were starting to get serious.

"Any questions?" he asked. When there was no response, he continued, "Right, then we'll go over the route one more time."

The briefing over, we headed for the airfield in the trucks.

"I'm beginning to feel like a real pilot," said Patricia as we made our way down to the airfield.

"You *are* a real pilot," said Connie, laughing. "What are you talking about?"

"Yes, I know, but I mean, a real pilot about to go into combat, just like the men do."

"We're just as good as any man," Shelly put in.

"And now we have the chance to prove it," I said. "That's the difference, isn't it, Patricia?"

"You see, Anna understands," Patricia said triumphantly.

"How was your date with the barman?" Maria asked Shelly, changing the subject.

"Oh ... well ... you know," said Shelly, smiling.

"We don't know, and that's why we want you to tell us!" said Maria.

"Later... I've got another bottle of gin," said Shelly with a laugh.

We arrived at the field and tumbled out of the trucks. The Mosquitos were waiting for us as usual. They were ably maintained by the technical crew, who watched us from a distance as we walked to our planes.

Once Maria and I were strapped in, I fired up the engines and waited for clearance.

"Bluebird Leader, take the flight out, you are clear to go," said Control over the radio.

"Roger," I replied.

I taxied to the end of the runway, eased back the throttle and let her go. The Mosquito picked up speed and our wheels left the ground. I circled the airfield, watching the others take off. Henry took off in the Spitfire so that he could fly above us, watching our progress.

When the last of the planes was airborne, I called the flight to order.

"Bluebirds, form up on me, close formation. We're about to go low-level flying. Take it easy and pay attention."

"Whoopee!" came the response from Patricia.

The others took up their places in the formation and I got the initial bearing from Maria. I dropped the kite as low as I dared, set the heading and started to open up the throttle.

Flying close to the earth is a completely different experience from flying at altitude. Things are suddenly fast, very fast. The ground rushes beneath you while things flash by on either side. Your whole focus is on what's up ahead.

We were hedge-hopping — dropping low and then hopping up and over obstacles. In some of the fields, we spooked the animals as we roared overhead. I felt bad for them, being a farm girl. I hadn't time to worry, though. We were eating up the ground at a cracking pace.

"Wow," said Maria after one perilous hop over a belt of trees. "This is pretty damn scary."

"No kidding," I replied. It was one thing carrying out aerobatics in a Tiger Moth, but this was something else entirely. I was glad of all the training we'd had so far.

"Imagine doing this over enemy territory," she said.

"I'm trying not to," I shot back as we approached a farmhouse. God only knew what the farmer must have thought as twelve Mosquitos roared over his roof.

As well as flying at a hell of a lick, I had to keep an eye on the flight and the formation. We had to keep our places. On a real attack, we couldn't afford for anyone to get lost or left behind. Besides which, we needed to strike in unison.

"This is not for the faint-hearted," said Maria as we flew up and over a farmhouse.

"Good job you're not then," I quipped.

"Beats the fairground rides any day," she shot back.

We hit each waypoint dead on target and turned to the next bearing. Some of these were quite sharp turns, testing our ability. We couldn't risk a wingtip hitting the ground. I tried to imagine what it would be like when we did this for real. How would we feel, flying into the teeth of the enemy?

"Anna, I said two zero five, two zero five... Anna!" Maria was shouting at me.

I had zoned out for a few seconds. I gave myself a mental shake. I couldn't afford to lose concentration, not now, when everyone was relying on me.

"Sorry," I said, turning the kite lightly onto the next heading.

"Keep your focus, Anna, come on!" Maria said fiercely.

I forced my attention back onto the terrain in front of us. Fields, hedges, trees, roads, all rushed by in a blur of green, brown and black.

Then, finally, we made the last waypoint and set a course for the airfield.

Suddenly, out of nowhere, a set of telegraph poles loomed up. They had been masked by a band of trees behind them. Now they were sharply in focus — and we were heading straight for them.

"Lines, lines, lines!" shouted Maria over the radio as we barrelled towards them at high speed. This was as much for the others as it was for me.

We had seen them just in time. I pulled up sharply, narrowly avoiding the poles, skimming over the top of the lines. I breathed a sigh of relief.

"Christ, that was close," said Maria.

"Have the others made it?" I asked her, unable to take my eyes off the front.

"I'll check… It looks like it… Oh…" Maria's voice died suddenly. The next moment my heart sank as the shout came over the radio.

"I've hit a bloody pole… Damn it… I can't control it… I'm going down…"

It was Jennifer.

"Break, Bluebirds, break," I said, throttling back and starting to circle around. I could see that Jennifer's Mosquito had hit a telegraph pole — one wing was half sheared off, and I watched in horror as her plane dived the short distance towards the ground. We weren't very high, and as luck would have it, her plane landed on its belly. But it didn't stop. The Mosquito started careening around and spinning as it headed towards the bank of trees.

Time slowed to a crawl. I watched as Jennifer's plane smashed into a hedge and finally come to a stop. I circled again with the rest of the flight, praying that she wasn't hurt.

To my immense relief, the canopy opened. Jennifer and Shelly climbed out and jumped down onto the ground. They started waving at us. Jennifer gave us the thumbs up.

"Thank goodness," I said, letting out a sigh of relief.

"Return to base, Bluebird Leader," said Henry. "Get Control to send someone to pick them up."

I turned my attention back to the fact I was still in charge of eleven planes, including my own. It was my job to get them home safe. A job which I now felt I had badly failed.

"Roger," I said to Henry, regaining my composure with difficulty. "Course?" I asked Maria.

She gave me the bearing and shot me a sympathetic smile. "Chin up, buttercup," she said quietly.

"Bluebirds, form up. Control, we've got a Bluebird down," I told the rest of the flight and the flight controller.

"Roger," said Control. "What's the position?"

Maria gave them Jennifer's coordinates. There was nothing more to be done. Reluctantly I flew back to base with Jennifer's aircraft receding into the distance behind me. I couldn't have done anything anyway. I was quickly learning that we had to do our duty no matter what.

One by one we landed. I taxied to our standing and killed the engine. For a moment I just sat there, taking in what had happened. I had let down my sister, the Air Force, and everyone on the flight. I felt like a failure.

"What's wrong, Anna?" Maria asked when I didn't move.

"I messed up. I'm not fit to lead this flight," I told her.

"Don't you *ever* say that," she said passionately.

"But I lost my focus. That could have been us. We could have been killed. Jenny could have died … and I would never forgive myself…"

I thought of what might have happened and how much worse it could have been. How would I face Father and Mother to tell them Jennifer was dead?

Maria was having none of it. "Stop it!" she said sharply. "Don't talk like that. You're doing a damn fine job."

"But I'm not."

I knew I had to pull myself together, yet I still felt the tears starting to run down my face.

"Oh, bloody hell," I said, angry with myself.

"We're just going to sit here," Maria said softly, "until you've composed yourself. Then we're going to go out, and you're going to act like the leader that you are."

"All right…" I said with a sniff.

Maria produced a handkerchief from her pocket and handed it to me wordlessly. I used it to dry my tears and blow my nose.

"Keep it," she said with a smile. "Now, do you feel better?"

"Yes," I said with a nod.

"Then let's go, Bluebird Leader."

I laughed weakly. We jumped down from the Mosquito and I tried to put on a brave face.

Henry walked up and looked at me keenly. No doubt my eyes were a little red from crying. If he noticed, he didn't mention it.

"Accidents happen," he said. "It's what you do afterwards that counts. We'll talk about it later."

"Yes, sir," I said.

"You're probably thinking you're not cut out to be the leader," he continued.

"Well —" I began.

"Well nothing," he said, cutting me short in a tone which brooked no argument. "You're leading this flight and that is not going to change." He nodded, then turned on his heel and left.

"You see," Maria said triumphantly. "I told you."

"I know," I nodded. "Where would I be without you?"

"You'd be right in it, and you know it," she laughed, and so did I.

Maria slipped her arm into mine and we walked back to the waiting trucks. Connie was leaning against the side of one of them and smoking a cigarette.

"That was a close shave," she said as we came up to her. "Oh, and Patricia nearly hit the lines as well."

"I did not," said Patricia indignantly.

"Did too," Connie shot back. "You only missed them because I shouted."

"It was all perfectly under control," said Patricia, putting on an air of innocence which made us all laugh.

The talk on the way back to Hawberry was all about the flight and the accident. I wondered how Jennifer had managed to hit the lines. Wasn't she paying attention?

When we arrived at the Hall, it was lunchtime.

"Go and get some grub," said Henry. "We'll have a debrief afterwards."

We piled into the dining room. I realised how hungry I was — I'd been running on adrenaline since we'd started the low-flying exercise. The ubiquitous pie, mash and veg were served up once more. I was grateful for it.

"Is this venison?" asked Connie as we tucked in.

"Tastes like it," I replied.

"Where on earth did they get it from?"

I was about to answer that the estate boasted a rather large herd of deer, when Jennifer and Shelly burst into the dining room.

"Jenny!" I cried, leaping up from my seat.

She came flying over, straight into my arms.

"Oh Jenny, darling, I thought you were…" I wanted to cry all over again.

"Dead? Well, I'm not," said Jennifer in her typically prosaic fashion.

"How did you…? What did you…?" I had so many questions I didn't know where to begin.

"How did I hit the telegraph pole?" she said. "I'll tell you when I've got some food. I'm famished."

Once she was seated and had had a few mouthfuls of food, she was ready to talk.

"Well?" I asked her, pushing my empty plate away. "How did it happen?"

"A moment of distraction," said Jennifer guiltily. "I was looking down at the instruments, just for a moment, and then Shelly was shouting about the lines and then she said—"

"There's a bloody great pole," Shelly cut in.

"And then we hit it," Jennifer continued.

"Oh God!" I exclaimed.

"Perhaps I *was* a bit low," Jennifer said, sounding contrite.

"A bit low?" said Shelly with a laugh. "I asked her if she was trying to mow the bloody grass, she was that close to the ground."

I hadn't noticed, of course. I had been focusing on flying my own plane.

"Jennifer, for goodness' sake," I said crossly. "You might have been killed. I was beside myself with worry when I saw what had happened."

"Oh, give over, Anna. I'm still here, aren't I?" Jennifer said, casually turning to Connie. "Have you got a smoke, love? I'm gasping for one."

"Sure."

Connie took one from a packet, put it in her mouth, lit it and then handed it to Jennifer, who puffed on it gratefully. That was Jennifer all over, so insouciant at times, and often, in my view, at the wrong times.

"Oh, Jenny," I said. "You always were a neck-or-nothing flyer, and this just proved it."

"Anna, it was a mistake, all right? It won't happen again," she said. She took a long pull on her cigarette and blew the smoke up into the air.

"Was she? A neck-or-nothing flyer?" asked Connie with interest.

"Yes, she was," I told Connie. "She took far more risks than I did when we were performing our flying circus stunts. I remember Daddy was always telling her off."

"There's no need to tell them all my peccadillos," said Jennifer, pretending to pout.

"Oh, but I want to hear them. Tell me more," said Connie, gleefully.

"Yes, go on," Shelly put in. "We all want to hear about it."

"Oh stop, all of you," Jennifer replied with a laugh.

I subsided. There was no point in telling Jennifer off. She would do exactly as she pleased regardless.

"All right," I said, closing the conversation. "But as your Flight Leader, Jennifer, I'm asking you to have a care in future and keep your eyes peeled when we're flying that low. Ask Shelly to read the instruments if you must."

"Yes, ma'am," said Jennifer, poking out her tongue.

"I'd say that counts as insubordination," Connie quipped.

"Oh, and what are you going to do about it?" Jennifer replied.

"I'm going to get some apple pie," Connie replied. "Do you want some?"

"Yes, please."

We all went up for dessert and ate it with relish. The conversation turned to the low-flying exercise. We all agreed it had been a pretty hair-raising experience.

"Better get used to it," I said. "We'll be doing it all over again soon enough."

We were given the afternoon off and to my surprise, the debrief was scheduled for the next morning. We were left at a loose end. At Shelly's instigation, the others decided to venture off the base to the local pub, the Dog and Trumpet.

Still shaken by the events of the day, I went to the house bar instead and ordered myself a glass of white wine. The bar was empty apart from some of the crew down at one end, conversing in loud tones. I sat at a table on my own, lost in my thoughts. There was much to think about — being away from home, the training, and of course the accident with Jennifer.

"Can I join you?" said a voice, breaking into my reverie.

I looked up. James was standing by my table. I smiled a little perfunctorily and shrugged. He sat down. He placed his glass of whisky on the table.

"All alone?" he asked me.

"As you see," I replied. "The others have gone off base."

He took a sip of his drink, savouring it. "So I gather. You didn't want to go with them?"

I was surprised he would know what we did when off duty. But the Sirens unit was his particular baby, so perhaps he kept a weather eye on us all.

"No, I'm not much of a socialiser," I replied. "I was usually found at home in the library, curled up with a book. Jenny's the one who likes to go out."

He laughed but then became a little serious. "Is it *just* that?"

He was certainly perceptive.

"No, it's not," I admitted. "What happened today … it shook me up a little, I suppose, especially since it involved my sister."

"You're close?" he asked, without passing comment on the crash. Something about his manner made me want to open up a little.

"Yes, we are."

It was true. Jennifer was everything to me. We had been inseparable from the moment she was born.

"And is there anyone else in your life?"

It was so lightly done that I didn't register it at first. Then I shot him a look. He wasn't interested in me, surely?

"I … no. There was, but we broke up," I said.

"I'm sorry," he said. "I didn't mean to pry. It's none of my business."

"It's all right. It was just one of those things. We weren't really in love…." I stopped and then blurted out an apology of my own. "Sorry, I'm not sure why I'm telling you all this. I mean, you're the CO."

"I'm not on duty just now," he replied, a faint smile playing on his lips.

"Didn't you say we were never off duty?" I couldn't help shooting his own words back at him. He had said it more than once in the many classes we'd taken over the preceding weeks.

"*Touché*," he laughed, acknowledging the hit. "I just like to get to know my people a little better, that's all."

"Oh … yes, I see."

The moment passed. We talked a little more about other things, and then I excused myself politely and went up to bed.

There had been something in the way he'd looked at me, I was sure. But I couldn't contemplate starting something with my CO; it would surely complicate things. I wasn't even sure if it was allowed.

I put it from my mind and went to sleep. Much later on I stirred as Jennifer slid under the covers beside me. I felt her arms go around me and hug me tight. Then, feeling a sense of peace, I slipped back into slumber.

CHAPTER SIX

"That was quite a night," Maria was saying as we sat together eating breakfast the following morning.

"Oh?" I took a sip of my tea.

"Shelly almost got into a fight because someone insulted Connie. Patricia had one over the eight and I thought she was going to end up dancing on the tables. We sang silly sentimental songs around the piano and just made it back by curfew," Maria informed me.

"Don't tell me any more," I said, laughing. "Really, I don't want to know."

"You should have come," said Jennifer.

"What *did* you do?" Maria demanded in her forthright way.

"I just had a drink in the bar," I said, addressing myself to my eggs on toast.

"On your own?" said Shelly with a smirk.

"Well, actually…" I found it awfully hard to lie, and I couldn't dissemble even though I wanted to. "James joined me for a drink, unexpectedly."

Naturally, it got taken up at once.

"Oh, you sly dog," Shelly said.

"It's always the quiet ones," added Patricia.

"It was just a drink!" I shot back, not wanting them to read anything more into it.

"Sure … of course," said Shelly in disbelieving tones.

Jennifer came to my rescue. "Leave her be," she said to the others, putting an arm around me protectively. "She's not going to start something with the CO, so you can cut that out, you lot!"

I shot my sister a grateful look and the others subsided. The conversation returned to their escapades at the pub and I was glad I had not gone.

With breakfast over, we repaired to the briefing room and waited for James to arrive. It was time to face the music for the accident of the previous day.

"Attention," said Gloria, entering the room.

As one, we stood and waited while James, Henry and the Marx Brothers followed her in. The two spies seemed to come and go quite a bit. I assumed they must be busy with other things besides the Sirens.

"At ease," said James, when they were all on the podium. The others took a seat, and the Marx Brothers lit up cigarettes.

We sat down and waited. I wondered what James was going to say. He and Henry had been very quiet on the subject of the crash up until now.

"We need to talk about yesterday," he said. "Firstly, accidents happen. A moment's inattention at high speed that close to the ground and you're most likely a goner. Fortunately, that was not the case yesterday."

Jennifer glanced at me with a guilty expression on her face. He had correctly divined the cause of the mishap.

"You cannot allow yourself to be distracted, even for a second," James continued. "SO Nightingale was lucky to survive the crash. It could so easily have been different, and by that, I mean fatal."

I looked at Jennifer and saw that she was a little pale now that she was forced to contemplate what could have happened. Perhaps it was a good thing; it might make her a little more careful in future. I squeezed her hand and she held onto it gratefully.

"So that's the first thing to take away from yesterday. You have to stay focused, particularly over enemy territory. We can't afford to lose planes, or our well-trained crew. As it is, we'll need to wait a day or two for a new Mosquito to be delivered. The second thing is this: if you do crash or are shot down on a mission, you cannot stop. You have to keep going and leave the plane behind."

A hand shot up.

"Yes, ASO Hartley?"

"But what if we do survive a crash? What are we supposed to do?" Pamela Hartley asked in her cut-glass voice.

James hesitated for a moment. He glanced at the Marx Brothers and Harpo gave him an imperceptible nod. "My colleagues from MI6 will answer your question."

Harpo and Chico stood up. They had been listening to James and smoking cigarettes in a leisurely fashion. The two of them stubbed out their smokes in an ashtray on a table behind them before speaking. "If you survive a crash over enemy territory, you could, of course, attempt to escape, find the Resistance and get back to Blighty," said Harpo.

"In theory," said Chico.

"But in practice, it's highly likely that you will be captured by the Germans. The one thing we can't have is you being captured in uniform. Although, of course, they'd be looking for male pilots and not female," Harpo continued.

"Can't we just change into civvies?" asked ASO Brenda Biggins, one of the navigators.

"You could, assuming you're not injured and assuming you had time," said Chico. "Assuming you could get away and find the Resistance, have the right papers and a whole lot of other things you might need, like fluency in French or Dutch…" He trailed off. That was a lot of assumptions.

"There is a very high chance you'll get picked up by the Germans, and if you are not in uniform you will be interrogated by the Gestapo as a spy. The counterintelligence network is extensive in Nazi Europe, and they have informants among the local population. Strangers will be reported to the authorities. If you happen to get shot down in Germany itself, then nobody is going to be your friend. If you are taken by the Gestapo, frankly, that's a place you don't want to be."

"We're going to tell you some things," Harpo said. "Unpleasant things. About what the Germans do to those suspected of being spies or part of the Resistance movements in Europe." He paused to allow us to absorb this. I wasn't sure I wanted to know, but he carried on. "The Gestapo have one aim and one aim only, and that is to gain all the information they can from the captured spy before killing them. A suspected spy will die, one way or another. They will use every method they can to extract what they want from you. First, it will be gentle persuasion and offers to let you go. Then will come threats and intimidation, about what will happen if you don't cooperate. If you still refuse to tell them what they want to know, the next part will not be pleasant…"

I closed my eyes, hoping he would spare us the details, but he did not.

"Let's begin with the simple stuff. Water torture. The victim's head is held underwater until they think they will drown. Then they are let up for air, asked for names, and it begins again, over and over until the will to resist is broken."

There was a collective gasp at this. None of us had really imagined it, but this was the brutal reality of war.

"If this doesn't work, then there are various other forms of torture they are likely to employ…"

I listened, horrified, to descriptions of beatings, broken bones, and more. It was awful, despicable. My horror was reflected in the faces of those in my squadron. The full consequences of what we had signed up for were finally starting to hit home. When he had finished, there was silence in the room.

"Why are you telling us all this?" Pamela said suddenly.

"Because that's the fate in store for you if you are captured, and you need to know."

"But the Geneva Convention," she protested. "Surely if we are in uniform, they can't do that to us."

"The British authorities will deny that you exist. And the enemy will believe you are a spy because British women do not fly planes into combat," said Harpo.

"We told you before you signed up that the Sirens are a secret squadron," said James. "Nobody will ever officially acknowledge the existence of this unit."

"If you are shot down," he continued, "you cannot be captured at any cost. Understand that. We will give you the means, but you will need to have the courage to use it."

The CO did not need to spell it out. There was only one outcome if you crashed — you had to die one way or another.

Nobody spoke. We were all in shock. Had we known what we were letting ourselves in for at the beginning, would we have still signed up? I didn't know, but I did know that we had a duty — a duty even unto death, and that was all there was to it.

"Let's be clear about one thing," James went on. "We are not training you for a suicide mission. We are *expecting* you to come back. We are *training* you to come back. We *want* you to come back. That's why we are working so hard to ensure you are the best you can be, so that you will come back and be ready to go again."

All of us breathed a collective sigh of relief on hearing this. It certainly made me feel a lot better. For a moment, it had seemed as if we really were expendable.

"We're talking about worst-case scenarios here," Henry put in. "Just remember that if something happens and your plane can still fly, then you must do your damnedest to make it back to Blighty. This unit needs you."

"All right," said James. "We've still got plenty to do. As soon as the replacement Mosquito arrives, we'll recommence low-flying training. I want you all to practise until you can do it with your eyes closed. Please don't take that literally."

There was laughter at this and the mood in the room lifted.

"When will our first mission be, sir?" asked Susan Bell.

"When you're ready," replied Henry.

"In the meantime, I'm sure you'll all be delighted to hear that you can assemble for drill practice, and then we'll go to the range for small arms fire," said Gloria.

There was a collective groan at this. We had to accept that regular drill was now part of our lives, although most of us enjoyed shooting the guns. I had used firearms on the farm, but this was different. It was more fun.

"That's all we need," said Shelly as we all filed out to the area which served as a parade ground. "More bloody marching."

"I guess it's penance for my crashing the plane," said Jennifer.

"Stop it, Jenny. We're all in this together," I said.

"Nobody blames you," said Connie. "It could have happened to any of us."

"Says who?" said Shelly.

We all turned to glare at her. She put up her hands placatingly.

"I'm joking, I'm joking."

"Come on," I told them. "Let's get to it."

"The Flight Leader has spoken!" said Shelly.

Maria rolled her eyes.

Nobody said any more. Sergeant Wallace was shouting instructions and we had to line up for drill.

The next couple of days passed quickly, and before long we were in the trucks heading out to the airfield once more. The replacement plane had arrived. We had a briefing from Henry beforehand.

"You're going to do low flying again," he said. "This time, you'll fly all the way down to the south coast and back at a low level. We're going to repeat this until you can do it confidently."

He proceeded to lay out the course on the map. Navigators were handed sheets containing waypoints and coordinates to follow.

"If there is another accident," he continued when this was done, "you are to continue flying and to radio in the coordinates, but under no circumstances are you to stop. Is that understood?"

There were murmurs of assent. James had pretty much drummed this message into us already.

"I want you to treat this exercise like a real mission," he said. "Fly as if your life depends on it."

With those words ringing in our ears, we were on our way. I looked at Jennifer. She was sitting next to Connie near the open back of the truck. They were sharing a cigarette. The smoke floated out of the opening. We both knew what the other was thinking. *Don't mess it up this time.*

"Here we go again," said Maria as the truck came to a halt and we all jumped out.

"Whose idea was it to come and join this unit?" said Shelly, following us.

"It was yours, if I recall it. It will be fun, that's what you said," Maria told her.

"Me and my big mouth," said Shelly with an exaggerated sigh.

"You love it really," said Patricia, laughing.

We reached our Mosquitos and I pulled the telescopic ladder down so that I could climb up through the side hatch.

Maria climbed up after me, pulled the hatch shut and strapped herself in.

"Ready?" I asked her.

"Ready," she said.

I fired up the engines and from then my attention was purely on flying. We went through the preflight routine and then I checked with Control.

"Control, this is Bluebird Leader requesting clearance," I said over the radio.

"Bluebird Leader, you're clear for take-off," came the response.

"Roger, thanks," I replied.

"Good luck, Bluebird Leader," said Control.

"Bluebird Flight, check-in," I said and waited for all of the pilots to tell me they were ready to go. After this, I gave the order for the off.

"All right, Bluebird Flight, let's go."

I taxied to the end of the runway, eased the throttle up, let off the brakes and the plane shot forward. I took off and circled the airfield with what was now practised ease. I was becoming familiar with the aircraft at last. I remembered what we had been told during instruction: the plane had to become an extension of ourselves; a single unit flying together. I was beginning to understand what that meant and recalled how I had felt much the same with the Tiger Moth after years of practice.

When all of the flight was airborne, we were ready to begin.

"Bluebirds, close formation, low-level flying," I said.

Maria confirmed the bearing. I dropped the kite as low as I could. Then I opened up the throttle. Once again, the ground flashed by below us.

"Keep your eyes on the terrain in front of you, pilots," I said.

"Wilco," said Jennifer, followed by the others. None of us wanted a repeat of last time.

Our route would take us on a flight path with Cambridge and then London on our left. We'd end up just past Chichester before flying back the same way.

For the most part, the route was over fields, but there were also small villages and towns we'd have to fly over at rooftop height. I didn't relish the thought. Maria was watching our progress like a hawk, my second pair of eyes.

This time around wasn't quite as nerve-racking. The hedges and trees slipped below us as I once again kept us as low as I dared, hopping over the obstacles. Without thinking, we developed a system where Maria would call out what was in front of us.

"Lines."

"Got it."

"House."

"Seen it."

"Tower."

"Yep."

I didn't know if anyone else did the same, but it worked for us. The coastal run was further than the last time, requiring concentration for longer. I could feel the adrenaline kicking in, aiding my heightened awareness. Then we hit our first town. My heart rate spiked.

I took us up to a height just above the rooftops.

"Hey," said Maria. "Don't knock anyone's chimneys off."

"I'm trying not to," I said with a laugh.

Below us, people stood in the streets, looking up as we flew overhead. We would be too fast for them to see much. We were there and gone in seconds. In hostile territory, this would be just as well. Someone could easily hit us with small arms fire if they were on the ball.

The town was behind us before we knew it, and we were back over the fields once more.

"Christ," said Maria. "That's one way to test your mettle."

"Are the others all right?" I asked her.

She flicked a glance left and right. "Yes, they're all with us, keeping at the same height."

Jennifer had been moved up to a position next to me, but her codename remained Bluebird Four. Henry had decided on the formation. Eventually, it would be me making those choices. Henry wasn't with us this time. He said we had to start flying the training runs alone. We were faster than his Spitfire in any case. We were on our own now, and all the decisions were down to me. This, I began to discover, was the burden of command.

"Town," said Maria as another small village loomed up before us. Then, "Lines, lines, lines."

Telegraph lines suddenly appeared, reminding us of Jennifer's crash. This time I acted quickly and so did the others. The flight rose above the lines as one body and flew over them with ease.

"Good job," said Maria.

"We're learning," I said.

We left the village behind us and within minutes we were over the Sussex Downs. Suddenly, the ground was no longer flat. It was punctuated by hills. I knew this would be a little more testing.

"Careful," said Maria as I started to climb, trying to keep parallel with the ground.

"I've got this," I told her.

"I bloody well hope so."

"Oh, ye of little faith."

The easy banter helped me focus. The hills gave way to fields with clumps of trees. We bypassed Chichester to our left and the next moment we were over water, heading for West Wittering beach. I dropped the kite low, skimming the waves. The water was thankfully reasonably calm, although the wind was picking up a bit from the sea.

Moments later we crossed the coastline and were over the Channel. I was just about to give the order to return when Susan Bell shouted out a warning.

"Bandits, bandits, nine o'clock."

This was all we needed, I thought, with a sinking feeling in my stomach. Maria and I peered over to our right. There were some planes in the middle-distance looming closer.

"Are those ours or theirs?" she said.

"I'm not waiting to find out," I told her, then over the radio, I said, "Bluebirds, return to base full throttle. Let's go!"

I banked the plane quickly and the flight wheeled around with me.

"They look like Focke-Wulfs," said Pamela.

"Damn it," I muttered.

"We don't know if they've seen us," said Maria.

"I'm not taking the chance," I replied firmly.

I took us a little higher than we had been flying before. Maria set a bearing directly back to Hawberry.

"Check whether they're following us," I told her.

She craned her head around, but there was a limited view out the back.

"See anything?" I asked.

"Not much, wait… Oh, bloody hell!"

"What?"

"They are getting closer."

The Mosquito was picking up speed after I had opened up the throttle. I knew we should be faster than the Wulfs.

"We'll outrun them," I said, trying to sound more confident than I felt.

Henry had told us not to attempt to engage fighters in a dogfight; they were far more manoeuvrable, and we would lose. That time I had shot down the Wulf was a fluke; he hadn't seen me coming or had seen me too late.

I decided to radio in our predicament. "Control, this is Bluebird Leader. We've picked up some bandits," I said.

"What's your position?" said Control.

Maria gave them the coordinates.

"We're heading back to base," I said. "Maximum throttle."

"Keep going, Bluebird Leader," Control replied.

"Is that all?" said Maria.

"What else are they supposed to do?" I asked her.

"Well, they could send some planes…"

"If we're over Europe, we'll be on our own," I shot back.

"But we're in Blighty."

She had a point, and I hoped that perhaps they might scramble a squadron in support.

"Check again," I said. "Try to see where they are."

She turned around awkwardly to look. "They're closer," she said.

"For goodness' sake!"

"Can't this thing go any faster?" she complained.

"I don't think so," I said.

"I knew that not going to church would do for me one day…" Maria lamented. I flicked her a glance, but she wasn't being serious. Humour was her way of coping with stressful situations.

"Just get us back to base," I said.

"You're the one flying this thing…"

"And you're the one navigating…"

I was wondering about perhaps gaining some height and whether it might help with the speed. If the Wulfs managed to get within firing distance, we were sunk. I put my attention back on the ground and watched it flying by below us. This was top speed and it seemed frighteningly fast.

Suddenly a squadron of Spitfires roared overhead. I had been so intent on flying that I hadn't seen them coming.

"Whoopee!" shouted Maria.

"Here comes the cavalry!" yelled Patricia.

"Bluebird Leader, a squadron's been scrambled," said Control.

"Roger. We've seen them, thanks," I replied. I breathed a sigh of relief. They would take care of the enemy. "Let's get back on course," I said to Maria.

"Wilco," she said, smiling.

She gave me a new bearing and I took the flight down lower once again. With the threat behind us, I throttled back a little and we made our way back to Hawberry without incident. After we landed, I taxied to our standing and killed the engine.

"Is this what it's going to be like?" said Maria. "On a real mission?"

"Probably … or worse," I said.

"Maybe I had better start going to church."

"That was a bloody close shave today," said Maria, sipping her glass of beer.

We were in the house bar, having a drink together. The others had informed me that if I wasn't going to go out with them, then they were going to stay in with me.

"Damn right," said Patricia. "Good job those Spitfires turned up."

"We were lucky," I replied. "Over enemy territory, we would have had no option but to outrun them."

"What's it going to be like, do you think? Flying an actual mission," said Connie, taking a drag on her cigarette then passing it to Jennifer.

"I think it will be exciting," said Jennifer.

"I think you've lost your bloody marbles," said Maria.

"A long time ago, darling, a long time ago," Jennifer agreed. She took a puff of the cigarette then passed it back to Connie.

"Where's Shelly anyway?" asked Patricia.

"Oh, she's out with her new beau," Maria told her.

"The barman?"

"Oh no, she's moved on since then. Apparently, this new man, Gary, is rather dashing," said Maria.

"Have you met him?"

"No, not yet."

"Talking of dashing…" Connie put in. She gestured over to the bar. James was standing there, talking to Henry. He saw me and smiled, then raised his glass in salute. I nodded back in acknowledgement.

"Ooh, looks like someone's got more than just a professional interest in you, Anna," said Maria.

"Stop it!" I told her, blushing furiously. "He's our CO, nothing more."

"Says you," Maria persisted in disbelieving tones.

"Let her be," said Jennifer, seeing my discomfort.

I couldn't understand how James discomposed me so much. It was true that he was handsome. I thought of Nigel. I'd never felt the same kind of flutter with him. It was strange and disconcerting. I was also acutely aware that he was my superior and as such he should be off limits. At least, that was what my head was telling me.

"I'm only teasing, you know that," said Maria, squeezing my hand affectionately.

"I know," I said, forcing my attention away from James. He had turned away in any case and resumed his conversation.

The rest of the evening passed pleasantly enough. James wasn't mentioned again. Jennifer and I were in our room getting ready for bed when Maria, Connie, Patricia and Shelly burst through the door.

"Shelly's upset and she won't tell us why," said Maria.

"What's happened?" I asked her.

"It's Gary," said Shelly, sitting down heavily on the bed. "He … he…"

Maria sat down beside her and put her arm around her. "Did he hurt you? God help him if he has," she said.

"No, no, nothing like that," said Shelly.

"Then what?"

Shelly's gaze shifted to the floor. "He … he's threatening to … to spill the beans about our unit," she said in halting tones.

"What!" I exclaimed.

"I know," she said, looking crestfallen.

"Shelly, tell me you didn't tell him about our unit?" said Maria crossly.

"Not in so many words… I had a bit too much to drink."

"Christ," said Maria. "You've signed the Official Secrets Act, for goodness' sake. You were sworn to secrecy. Now you've jeopardised this whole operation."

"I know. I'm sorry, I didn't mean to."

"Didn't mean to?" Her friend rounded on her. "You've put this whole unit and everyone in it in danger, not to mention the fact that you could go to prison!"

Shelly burst into tears. In a flash, Jennifer was beside her, comforting her navigator. My sister was nothing if not compassionate.

"Look," said Patricia, interjecting. "Instead of getting angry with Shelly, let's work out what we're going to do about it."

"What do you mean?" Maria shot back. "What *can* we do about it?"

"We can stop him from talking…"

"How?" I asked her, nonplussed.

"Let's think about it," said Connie. "Let's think about how we could persuade him."

"I'll persuade him all right," said Maria, firing up.

"Not that way," said Patricia, divining Maria's thoughts. "It's got to be something … like a matter of life and death."

We thought for a few moments. Patricia stood with her arms folded, staring up at the ceiling as if she was deep in thought. Then suddenly she looked at us and snapped her fingers. "I've got it," she said.

"What?" Connie asked her.

"We're going to need Susan Bell," Patricia continued.

"Susan? Why?"

"Because she can fly a B-17."

We all stared at her as if she had completely lost her senses.

"What the hell has a B-17 got to do with it?" asked Maria.

Patricia turned to Shelly, who had regained a little of her composure. "Shelly, what exactly *did* you tell Gary?"

"We were just talking," she began. "Gary asked me what I do. So, I gave him the usual stuff about transporting planes. And he said, 'Is it really just that?', and I said, 'Wouldn't you like to know?'"

Maria snorted on hearing this and rolled her eyes.

"He kept pushing and I told him it was top secret," Shelly continued. "Of course, that was the wrong thing to say."

"You think?" said Maria.

"He kept on and on. Then he said if I didn't tell him, then he'd speak to my commanding officer and tell him how I'd slept with him in the barn down the road."

"Oh, Shelly, you didn't!" said Connie.

"Yes, and it will be seen as conduct unbecoming and I'll be sent home," Shelly wailed.

I tried to regain control of the situation; I was Flight Leader, after all. "Did you or did you not tell him what our unit does?" I asked Shelly.

She shook her head. "Not in so many words."

"What words *did* you use?" I persisted.

"I said it wasn't just transporting planes, it was much more than that, but it was top secret. Now he's insisting I tell him the whole of it."

"Why?" asked Jennifer. "Is he a spy?"

"No, he's a reporter. He wants the story."

"That's even worse!" said Maria with a groan.

Patricia held up her hand for silence. "Well, we need to change his mind about that, don't we? So let me tell you my plan."

When she had finished, we all stared at her.

"Anyone got a better idea?" she asked. "Other than going to the CO and getting Shelly thrown out of the Sirens?"

"When are we going to do it?" I said, becoming practical.

"That's the spirit," said Patricia. "In a couple of days' time. That should be long enough to get things arranged."

"All right," I said. "Shelly, you need to pretend you're going to spill the beans. Set up a rendezvous with Gary. We'll do the rest."

"Will do," she replied eagerly. I had no idea if Patricia's outlandish scheme would work, but it was worth a shot. The only problem was that all our necks would then be on the line.

CHAPTER SEVEN

The next two days flashed past almost as quickly as the ground under our Mosquitos during low-level flying. There were no further incidents and the practice runs went off smoothly. We didn't see any enemy aircraft. Nobody got themselves into difficulty. I considered that to be a positive indication we were improving. It seemed I wasn't the only one.

At the end of another practice session, I returned to Hawberry to be greeted by James.

"Things are going very well, I gather," he said, smiling.

"Yes, sir, they are," I said, trying to quell the flutter in my chest at being quite so close to him. This was happening with annoying regularity.

"You're doing a damn fine job, Anna. You'll all soon be mission fit," he continued. "Just as I'd hoped."

"Thank you, sir," I replied.

"Keep it up," he said. "I've got plans for you … for all of you." He tagged on the last bit after giving me a meaningful look.

I watched him walking away and Maria sidled up to me.

"Getting cosy?" she said.

"Just talking," I replied defensively. "James was telling us what a good job we're doing."

"Good thing he doesn't know what we're up to later," said Maria with a laugh.

Lunch dragged on for all of us. There was an air of anticipation in our little group.

"Come on," said Patricia as soon as we'd finished. "Let's get going."

I had let her take charge, as it was her plan. She had made all the arrangements. She led us out into the car park and we piled into one of the trucks. I sat up front with Patricia. Maria was driving. The others were in the back.

"How did you manage to get hold of a truck?" I asked Patricia as we pulled away.

"I said we needed it for an afternoon out," she said. "It was easy enough."

"She slipped the transport commander a bottle of rum," Maria added.

We drove out of the estate, passing the sentries without any problems. It seemed they were quite familiar with the comings and goings of my fellow Sirens. So much so that Maria was on first-name terms with some of them.

Not far down the road lay a hotel. We dropped Shelly off there and drove around the corner to wait. Her rendezvous with Gary was in one of the rooms. We gave them half an hour or so to get settled before making our move.

"It's time," said Patricia, looking at her watch. Maria parked the truck out the front.

Shortly afterwards, Jennifer, Patricia, Connie, Maria and I found ourselves in a room adjoining the one next to Shelly's. We could hear Shelly and Gary talking through the adjoining door. I looked at Patricia. She gave us the thumbs up.

Connie pulled a revolver from her pocket. I stared at it in alarm. I didn't remember discussing the use of firearms.

"Where did you get that?" I hissed.

"From the armoury," she told me quietly.

"How?"

"I said it was for firearms practice — also I slipped the armourer a bottle of whisky," she replied with an insouciant shrug. "But don't worry. I'm not planning on shooting anyone."

"I thought we were going to overpower him," I said to Patricia, still not entirely happy with this turn of events.

"Change of plan," she said. "This is a much better idea."

I wasn't sure I agreed with her, but there was no time to argue. Connie positioned herself by the door, and Patricia put her hand on the handle. She turned it softly and the door swung open.

We entered the adjoining room to find Shelly wrapped in an amorous embrace with Gary. They were in the bed and both appeared to be naked. Gary turned around as we entered and stared at us, then at the revolver Connie had aimed in his direction.

"Who the hell are you?" he said. "Why are you pointing a gun at me, for Christ's sake?"

"Softly," Patricia told him. "Not so loud."

Shelly pulled the blanket up to cover herself and winked at us.

"What the hell do you all want?" he said.

"We're friends of Shelly," said Patricia. "We just want to have a little chat."

"What about?" he demanded. "What right have you to come bursting in like this?"

Patricia was implacable. "Get dressed. We need you to come with us."

Gary shook his head and looked defiant. "And if I don't? What will you do, shoot me?"

Connie entered the fray at this point. "Yes," she told him.

He blenched a little. "You won't do that," he said, though without quite so much bravado.

Connie was made of sterner stuff. "Try me," she said, pulling back the hammer on the gun.

"Wait, you can't just shoot me. That would be murder." His voice took on a note of desperation.

"You're a spy," said Patricia. "We've got friends in very high places. Believe me, it won't be seen as murder."

Gary looked wildly about him, but there was no means of escape. Jennifer had moved to cover the door. The rest of us were standing by the door to the adjoining room.

"I'm not a spy," Gary protested, still looking to bluff his way out of it.

He hadn't counted on Connie. She looked him straight in the eye and shifted her aim a little. He stared at the barrel of the gun.

He put his hands up in surrender. "All right, all right, just let me get dressed."

Connie moved back a little to give him room but kept the gun levelled at his chest. Shelly shot us a grateful smile and slid off the bed.

Once they were both properly attired, Patricia said to Gary, "You are coming with us and if you try anything, you're dead, understood?"

Gary nodded his acquiescence.

"Actually," said Jennifer to Gary, "put your hands behind your back — there's a good boy."

She produced a pair of handcuffs from her jacket pocket and proceeded to snap them on his wrists. She fished in her pocket again and brought out some black armbands with the letters MP on them in red. She passed them around so that we could put them onto our arms. The escapade was turning out to be full of surprises.

"Where did you…?" I began.

"Don't ask," she replied. "I just thought it would be easier if we looked the part."

"Let's move," said Patricia when we were ready.

Connie pocketed the gun, saying to Gary, "Don't think I won't use this if I have to."

He didn't reply. Two of us went in front of Gary and the rest behind. Connie made sure she was directly behind him.

In this fashion, we proceeded to walk down the corridor and out through the lobby of the hotel. The clerk at the desk looked up in alarm when he saw us.

"We're from the Military Police," Patricia informed him airily. "We're arresting this man for going AWOL."

"Oh … right," said the clerk, and turned his attention back to the paper he was reading. Once we were in the car park, we made Gary lie down in the back of the truck.

"Where are you taking me?" asked Gary.

"Shut it," said Connie.

"Put a blindfold on him," said Jennifer.

I left them to it and shut the tailgate. Then I climbed into the front along with Maria and Patricia.

We drove back to Hawberry Hall and passed through the gate without incident once again. Maria turned the truck down the road towards the airfield. All was quiet in the back. Connie was obviously keeping Gary compliant.

After a few minutes, we arrived. At the end of the line of Mosquitos sat a B-17 bomber. It was there purely for show, to keep up the pretence that Hawberry was an air transport base. Up until now, we had never used it.

Susan Bell was an ex-ATA pilot who knew how to fly many different planes, including the Flying Fortress. As we got closer, I could see her sitting up in the cockpit. She gave us a wave. Maria backed the truck up to the aircraft so that the entrance hatch was obscured from the control tower.

She killed the engine. We jumped down and went around to the back of the truck.

"Let's get him in the plane," said Patricia.

"Come on," said Connie to Gary, who was still lying on the floor. "Upsidaisy."

"Where are you taking me?" Gary asked, getting up onto his knees. He was now sporting a blindfold.

"You'll find out soon enough," she told him.

The entrance hatch to the plane was on one side, accessed by pulling yourself up into it. It was rather like the Mosquito in that respect. Susan must have found a ladder to make it easier to get Gary in. We pushed him up the ladder with some complaints from him and then followed him up. There was a small space behind the pilot's seat, not large enough for all of us, so we led him through the narrow bomb bay and into the rear compartment where there were more seats, forcing him to lie on the floor once more.

"You go and sit up front with Susan," Patricia said to me. "We'll manage here until it's time."

"Time for what?" Gary asked, hearing this.

"Never you mind," Patricia told him.

He subsided. I couldn't imagine what was going through his head, but I didn't have a lot of sympathy for his predicament. I returned through the bomb bay to the front and sat in the co-pilot's seat. I put on the headset.

"Hi," said Susan. "Ready for our little joyride?"

"I guess," I replied.

"Relax, it'll be a breeze. I'll do all the flying."

She started up the engines one by one. Once they were turning nicely, she spoke on the radio. "Control, this is Eagle One, requesting permission to take off," she said.

"Roger, Eagle One. Just hold while we check your clearance," said Control.

"Damn, that wasn't supposed to happen," Susan muttered under her breath, then, louder, "Roger, Control, I'll just taxi to the runway and wait." She let the brakes off and the plane started to move.

"What did you tell them about flying this plane?" I asked her.

"Oh, just that we'd been asked to fly it to another airbase. They said it wasn't on the flight roster, but I said someone must have forgotten, you know — last minute thing."

This didn't sound plausible. Control was pretty hot on protocol as far as I knew.

"It'll be fine," she said. "Don't worry. We'll get airborne one way or another."

The Flying Fortress made its way to the end of the runway with her expert hands guiding it lightly on the controls. I could tell Susan was well practised as a pilot.

We reached the end of the runway and Susan began to wind up the engines.

"Control, Eagle One, ready for take-off," said Susan.

"Eagle One, please hold. We're still getting clearance," said Control.

I looked at Susan and she looked at me. This didn't sound good. Susan wasn't about to be thwarted.

"Control, please repeat," she said. "You are breaking up." She tipped me a wink.

"Eagle One," said Control. "Do not take off, I repeat, do not take off."

"Wilco," said Susan, as if she had not heard correctly. "Taking off."

"No, do *not* take off," came the instant response.

"Roger, we're on our way, thanks again," said Susan, opening up the throttles and letting off the brakes.

"Eagle One, you do not have clearance, Eagle One…"

Susan calmly reached forward and clicked off her radio. The wheels left the ground and the next moment we were airborne.

"What will happen now?" I asked her.

"Oh, they might send someone up after us, so you might want to get done what you need to do fairly pronto."

She took the bomber into a steep climb to just under fifteen thousand feet, then she set a level course away from the airfield.

"We're at the limit we can fly without oxygen," she told me. "Go and do what you've got to do."

I jumped down from the pilot cockpit and headed back to the others.

"We don't have much time," I said to Patricia. "They didn't clear us for take-off, but we did it anyway. It's likely they'll send a plane after us very shortly."

"All right," said Patricia. "Let's get busy."

"I'll get the bomb bay doors," said Jennifer, going forward to the bombardier's section where the bomb bay switch was located. In a few moments, the doors opened. I could see the land far beneath us as I peered through the hatch into the bay.

"It's showtime," said Patricia.

"All right, you," Connie said to Gary. "Get up."

"What's going on? What are you doing?" he said, the panic now evident in his voice.

Between us, we got him to his feet and manoeuvred him onto the narrow bomb bay walkway. When he was in the middle of the bay, Patricia took hold of one of his arms and Connie the other. He was still in handcuffs and couldn't hold on to anything.

"What are you doing?" he began to shout in alarm, feeling the wind rushing up through the open bay.

"Take off his blindfold, then he can see exactly what we're doing," said Patricia.

Although there were rails on either side of the walkway, it was very precarious. I was standing by Patricia, holding on to her, and Shelly was holding on to Connie, just in case. Jennifer was holding on to me and Maria was holding Shelly.

As soon as Patricia took off Gary's blindfold, he began to scream.

"What are you doing?" he shouted, looking down through the open bay. "What the hell are you doing?"

"Shut up," said Patricia calmly. "And listen."

"Get me off here, get me off!" he yelled, ignoring her.

"With pleasure," said Patricia. "One slip and you'll be down through that hole. You'll drop fifteen thousand feet until you hit the ground. What do you think will happen then, Gary? Hmm?"

"You can't do this!" Gary screamed.

Connie's voice cut through his hysteria. "Shut up and listen, or we'll drop you right now!" she said. "Is that what you want?"

Gary stopped screaming and shook his head. It was finally borne in on him that we meant business.

"Now, you listen to me," said Patricia, once he was silent. "You thought you could blackmail Shelly — well, this is what happens when you betray the sisterhood."

"What sisterhood? What are you talking about?" said Gary, momentarily diverted.

"I'm talking about *us*. You try to hurt one of us, you hurt all of us. Now, did you or did you not try to blackmail Shelly?"

Gary's face fell. His bravado had finally left him. "Yes, yes, I did… I'm sorry, I didn't mean it."

"Are you a spy?" Connie asked him.

"What?"

"Are you a bloody spy? Answer the question!" she shot back at him.

"No, I'm not. I swear I'm not."

Pamela went in for the kill. "Swear on your life that you'll keep your bloody mouth shut about Shelley and anything she told you. Otherwise, we'll be obliged to drop you off for that happy landing."

Gary's voice took on a pleading tone. "Please no, I swear, I won't tell a soul. Just let me go, please, please, for God's sake."

We let him stew for a bit longer while he shut his eyes tight, not wanting to look down. Finally, Patricia put him out of his misery.

"All right, but if you breathe a word about any of this, we'll come and find you. And next time we won't be so nice."

There wasn't any more we could do. If nothing else, we'd put the fear of God into him about what we might be capable of.

"Let's go," Patricia said, relenting at last. "Take him back."

Gary looked visibly relieved as Connie pulled him back into the crew section. It was done. Jennifer went to close the bomb bay doors and I headed back to the cockpit.

"How did it go?" Susan asked as I resumed my seat.

"Pretty well, all told. He was completely terrified."

She started to laugh. "I wish I'd seen it. Uh-oh." She flicked a glance sideways. I looked too and there was a Spitfire on our wing. "I guess we've been rumbled," she said.

She leaned forward and put her radio back on. As soon as we did so, it crackled to life.

"Eagle One, I don't know what you're playing at but bring that bloody bomber back to base now, do you read me?"

It was Henry and he didn't sound happy. There was nothing else for it but to comply.

"Roger, I read you. Heading back as requested," Susan told him.

"And who is that with you?" he demanded.

"It's SO Anna Nightingale," she said.

"I see. Well, get the plane on the ground, then we will discuss what you're doing up here. You can follow me in."

"Wilco," said Susan.

The Spitfire flew on towards Hawberry.

"That wasn't in the plan," I said to Susan.

"No," she sighed, turning the bomber to follow Henry's flight path.

"Control, this is Eagle One requesting clearance to land," she said as she lined up our approach.

"Eagle One, you're clear," said Control.

Susan had it all in hand. I had a heavy heart. Was this end of my Air Force career? I had not realised how much I'd come to love being part of the Sirens. Now it was very possibly going to fall apart.

CHAPTER EIGHT

We landed the plane and I could see there was something of a welcome party as we taxied to the standing.

"Looks like we're in the bloody basket now," said Susan. "It was nice knowing you."

"You too."

The others came out through the bomb bay again and one by one we jumped down from the plane. Gary got down with difficulty, since he was still in handcuffs. As we stood in front of the aircraft, we were approached by James, Gloria, Henry and what appeared to be an armed escort.

I blenched at the sight of them, wondering why James had felt that was necessary.

"Quite a few of you, I see," James remarked, seemingly unruffled by our appearance.

"Yes, sir," I said, stepping forward and saluting.

"And who is that?" he asked, indicating Gary.

"That's someone who was attempting to blackmail ASO Cartwright, sir," I said.

"Hey!" said Gary. "I made a promise! What the hell is wrong with you?"

James looked him up and down with seeming distaste. "Take him into custody," he said to the escort. "We'll decide what to do with him once he's been questioned."

"I'm not a spy! What's the matter with you people?" Gary said, objecting at once to this plan.

"You'll get a chance to have your say," said James. "If these officers have got you handcuffed, then I suspect there's a very good reason for it." He turned to the sergeant in charge of the escort. "Take him away!" he ordered.

"As for the rest of you," said James, as we watched Gary go, "I'll meet you back at the Hall, and then you can tell me what this is all about."

"Yes, sir," we said.

He turned on his heel with Henry and left.

We were somewhat subdued as we climbed into the truck. Gloria drove it, and I sat in the front beside her with Maria.

"Don't be fooled by James's calm demeanour," Gloria said as we drove. "He's not happy, believe me."

"Is he very angry?" I asked.

Gloria laughed. "Oh, he's not angry. You don't want to see that. Let's just say he's tremendously displeased, so I hope you've got a good explanation."

"We've got an explanation," I replied. "I'm not sure it's a good one."

"Just be truthful with him, Anna. That's by far the best way."

Having dispensed that advice, she said no more. I glanced at Maria and she squeezed my hand. I smiled wanly. Displeasing James made me feel unaccountably dreadful.

When we arrived at Hawberry, Gloria led us through a maze of corridors to a large room we hadn't seen before. It was lined with wainscoting, had pictures on the wall and was covered in gilded mouldings. There was a marble fireplace on one side. A large table ran almost the full length of the room, with chairs tucked neatly underneath.

James was seated at one end, along with Henry. I assumed that this must have been the original dining room. Gloria bade us all to take a seat.

"Right," said James. "Will one of you please tell me what this is all about?"

"Sir…" I began, but Shelly cut me off.

"Let me, Anna. This is all my fault, after all."

"Go ahead," said James. "I'm all ears."

"Gary, sir, he's my boyfriend," said Shelly.

"The man in handcuffs is your boyfriend?"

"Well … he *was* my boyfriend until…"

To James's credit, he listened to Shelly's story without interruption. When she told him about Gary blackmailing her, he stopped her.

"Did you, in fact, tell him what this unit does?" he asked.

"No, sir. I just said it was more than transporting planes, and then he kept pressing me for information."

"Which you didn't divulge?" he said. "Truthfully?"

"No, sir. I said it was top secret…" She trailed off.

"Probably not very sensible, was it?" he said mildly.

"No, sir."

"So," James said, looking around the table, "after Shelly told you all about this blackmail attempt, whose idea was it to handcuff Gary and take him up in the B-17?"

"It was mine, sir," said Patricia.

"Let's hear it then."

"I thought we needed to scare him, that's all. We didn't want the unit to be jeopardised," said Patricia. "So, I worked out a plan which we thought was foolproof at the time…"

Once again, James remained impassive as she finished the tale, although his mouth twitched more than once when she related the part about threatening to drop Gary out of the bomb bay.

"So let me get this straight," said James. "You bribed the transport I/C with alcohol to get the truck and then the armourer with whisky to obtain a weapon, and somehow got hold of a pair of handcuffs and MP armbands. And then," he continued, "you took a B-17 up without permission and you threatened to throw a civilian out of the aircraft. Is that about the size of it?"

No one spoke. It sounded as bad as it was.

"It was certainly an enterprising plan, I'll give you that," said James. "I have to admire your resourcefulness in actually carrying it out. But why didn't you just come to me with the problem in the first place?"

"Because we didn't want Shelly to get thrown out of the Sirens," I replied.

"So you placed yourselves in a position where I could justifiably have the whole lot of you expelled from this unit." He paused. "If I was inclined to do so."

"So, you're not…" I began.

"We've spent a good deal of time and money training all of you. And you are all turning into first-class pilots and navigators."

He paused to look at us. I was feeling contrite and I was sure the others were too, judging by their expressions.

"I'm unhappy that you didn't trust me enough to come and tell me that you had made a mistake. Or Henry or Gloria, for that matter. We're not ogres. We've bet our careers on the Sirens, and if you think that some hare-brained stunt is going to get in the way of the success of this unit, you are very much mistaken," he said.

"Thank you, sir," I said.

"I haven't finished," he continued. "Having said that, I can't allow this to go unpunished. So, you are all confined to the base for the next two weeks, on top of which you will spend the next three days doing drill all day. After that, you can resume your duties. Next time, remember to come to me first."

All of us thanked him in turn.

"What will happen to Gary?" asked Shelly, emboldened by the fact we had got off quite lightly.

"He'll be questioned by MI6, and then we'll decide what to do with him," said James. "Any other questions?" When nobody spoke, he said, "Then you are all dismissed except Anna."

Maria shot me a look of reassurance. I wondered what he wanted to say to me. The others all filed out, leaving the two of us alone.

"Anna," James said when they had gone. "Your actions today were not exactly those of a Flight Leader, as well-intentioned as they might have been. You know that, don't you?"

I fired up at once. "These women are my sisters, sir. I will protect them at all costs, no matter what. That is what a Flight Leader does."

"Which is commendable," he said with a smile. "But you also have a duty to the Air Force and to this squadron as a whole. Duty comes first."

He was right, of course.

"Are you standing me down?" I asked him bluntly.

"Should I?" he asked me with equal frankness.

"I'm a bloody good leader, sir," I said.

He raised an eyebrow and when he looked at me, he really did look so very attractive. It was wholly distracting.

"What you did was reckless in so many ways. You contravened a lot of regulations and yet…"

"And yet?" I said, regarding him steadily.

"And yet those same qualities make you the outstanding leader you are… Does that answer your question?"

My ire cooled at once. "Yes, sir, thank you."

"You're welcome. Then … perhaps we could share another drink sometime?" he ventured.

"Perhaps we could," I said. "Was there anything else, sir?"

"No, that's all. You may go."

I stood up and saluted him. He returned it with a smile. As I walked towards the door, he called after me.

"Anna," he said. "I'm not asking you to change."

I hesitated with my hand on the door handle. Then I inclined my head slightly in acknowledgement and left. My mind was in a whirl.

As I started to walk back to my room, the dinner gong sounded. I rounded a corner and was ambushed by the others, all clamouring to know what had transpired.

"Woah, ladies, please. One at a time," I said.

"Well, what did the CO say?" Maria demanded.

"He said my actions weren't those of a Flight Leader," I began.

"What!" said Maria furiously.

"I'm going right back in there to give him a piece of my mind," said Connie with a belligerent light in her eye.

"Hang on," I said, gently restraining her. "Then he said I was an outstanding leader just the same."

"You can't just leave it there," said Shelly.

"I'll tell you over dinner. I'm starving," I said with a laugh.

"James likes you," said Jennifer later when we were back in our room. We were lying in bed together.

"Maybe, but he's our CO."

"So what?"

"Well, it's a big deal, don't you think?"

"Do you like him?"

"What does it matter if I do? I don't see how we could ever be together."

"Love will find a way — isn't that what Mummy says?"

"I'm not in love with him," I told her, turning away.

She pulled in close, wrapping her arms around me. "If you say so."

"Have you ever been in love, Jenny?" I asked her sleepily.

"Yes, I think so."

"I never have…"

"Not with Nigel?"

"Definitely not with Nigel."

"You will be, darling, one day, and it will be the most glorious thing you've ever felt in your life."

My eyes closed on her words. I wondered who she had loved so deeply to be able to say that.

CHAPTER NINE

"Three days of drill is more than enough for anyone," said Shelly as our little cadre sat together in the bar a few nights later.

"I'd had it after one day," said Connie, taking a drag on her cigarette and passing it to Jennifer.

"If I hear Sergeant Wallace say 'order arms' one more time..." Maria rolled her eyes.

I laughed. In a way, the 'punishment' had brought us all closer. Perhaps that was the point.

"Anyone know what happened to Gary?" asked Susan Bell. She had now joined our little band since she had become a *de facto* co-conspirator. Tagging along was her navigator, Pamela. I assumed she might be from aristocratic stock, but she was a good sport.

"Hopefully they dropped him out of a plane after all," said Shelly, who was unrepentant.

My attention was caught by Henry, who had wandered over to our table.

"Hello, ladies," he said. "Have you enjoyed your little sojourn?"

"What do you think?" said Connie.

He laughed. "We'll be glad to have you back," he said. "I'm sure you're going to enjoy the next few days."

"Why's that?" asked Jennifer, tapping her cigarette on the ashtray.

"Oh, you'll see. But if you like blowing things up..." He trailed off.

"Hey, you can't just leave us hanging like that," Patricia complained.

"See you all in the morning," he said. "Enjoy the rest of the evening." He nodded pleasantly to us all and walked away before anyone else could say anything.

"Blowing things up?" said Susan. "Now that sounds like fun."

The following morning, we assembled after breakfast in the briefing room. I was more than happy to be there and determined that we wouldn't put another foot out of line if I could help it.

James, Henry and Gloria were up on the podium as usual.

"You're probably all wondering when you're going to see some action," said James.

Suddenly everyone was listening intently.

"The next few days are key," he continued. "You are going to perform strafing and bombing exercises with live ordnance in preparation for a mission."

Pamela piped up immediately. She was one of the most vocal members of our squadron. "What's the mission, sir?" she asked.

"I can't tell you that yet," he said. "Suffice it to say that once these exercises are completed, all will be revealed."

"Assemble on the airfield in flying gear in thirty minutes," said Henry.

"Dismissed," said James.

As the others filed out of the room, I made my way up to the podium. James was talking to Gloria but turned when he saw me.

"Anna?"

"Sir, some of us were wondering … erm … what happened to Gary," I said.

"Ah, yes, Gary," he replied. "Why don't you come and see me after practice? I'll tell you then."

My stomach did a few flips at the thought of being alone with him.

"You can bring Shelly if you like," he continued, as if sensing my hesitation. "He was her beau, after all."

"All right, sir. I'll do that."

"See you later, then," he said, turning back to Gloria.

I went to join the others with mixed emotions. Every time I was in his presence I felt flustered. I quelled my feelings with an effort and focused instead on the forthcoming training. Bombing things with live ordnance did sound rather fun.

We assembled in one of the hangars and Henry briefed us in a group. There was a large map on a stand. He went over the flight path and target, which was marked out on a bombing range.

"You've done this before, but not with live bombs," he said. "It's completely different to dropping a cement-filled lump of metal. For a start, if you're too close when the bomb goes off, you're going to be caught by the blowback from the blast."

It was a sobering thought.

"We are doing a low-level bombing run, as you have already done in exercises," he said. "The fuses on the bombs are timed exactly. You will make the run in a line, keeping a precise number of seconds between you. That means that the plane dropping the bombs will be out of range when they go off, and the plane behind it will be far enough away not to get caught in the blast before they come in and drop theirs. Does everyone understand?"

We replied in the affirmative. We would fly away from the range target and then come back in a low-level run. I would naturally lead the run.

"All right, then get to it," he said.

We walked out to the Mosquitos in a group. I started mentally preparing myself for the run. The reality of an actual mission was getting closer. The ground teams had loaded the ordnance; all we needed to do was fly it in. Henry was going up in the Spitfire to observe us.

As we walked in silence, Connie smoked the last bit of her cigarette and threw the butt onto the grass.

"Good luck," she said to us as she and Patricia headed for their plane.

"It's not about luck," Maria shot back. "It's about doing it right."

"Sure, I know, but a bit of luck always helps," said Connie, and Maria laughed.

We climbed into our plane and strapped in. I looked at Maria as she closed the hatch.

"Are we ready for this?" I asked her.

"Are you?" she said.

"As ready as I'll ever be."

"Then let's do it."

I fired up the engines and waited until the rest of the flight was ready. As always, I had them all check in before setting forth.

"Control, this is Bluebird Leader requesting permission to take off," I said.

"Bluebird Leader, you're clear," said Control.

"Roger," I replied and then, "Bluebirds, here we go."

That was the signal. I opened up the throttle and taxied down to the end of the runway, followed by the other planes. I wound up the engines and the next moment we were airborne. It was always a glorious feeling, the moment the wheels left the ground. Maria gave me the bearing and I circled around the airfield, waiting for the rest of the flight.

The last Mosquito took off and I gave the order. "Bluebirds, close formation, form up."

The other planes settled on each side of us, then I wheeled the flight away from the airfield. We flew several miles from the target range to allow for a realistic approach. The sky was reasonably clear and there was thankfully little wind. I was feeling confident that things would go well for this first live bombing practice.

I looked around but I didn't see Henry; he was no doubt circling somewhere above us. He kept out of the way because this was my flight. My watch. My responsibility. We reached the waypoint. I took a deep breath.

"This is it," I said to Maria.

"Yes," she said, and gave me the bearing for the target.

Even though it was a practice run, it felt real.

"Bluebirds, single attack formation, low-level flying," I said, peeling off and taking the kite as low as I could. The others would follow me one by one at timed intervals.

Once more, the ground rushed under us. My attention was fixed on the terrain in front and then finding the target. Each plane had to fly over the target behind me at an exact number of seconds. We would be stretched out in a line. The following planes would be able to see me and keep to the line I was flying. It ought to be simple.

We started up our hazard-spotting routine as the terrain flashed by.

"House," said Maria as a farmhouse loomed up before us.

"Seen it."

"Pole."

"Got it."

The familiar patterns kicked in after so many hours of constant training. I hopped up and over just as we'd done before. It was becoming second nature. Even so, I could feel my heart thumping faster. Something about the fact I was carrying live ordnance focused my mind.

"Target in five," said Maria as we approached a flat swathe of land which constituted the firing range.

"Can you see it?" I asked her.

"No."

We flew on, straining for a sight of the target.

"In four," she said.

We weren't quite at maximum speed, but it was fast enough to be coming up rapidly on our objective. I had to release the bombs at the correct moment — that was key.

"In three."

"Where is it?" I wondered out loud, straining to see.

"In two."

Henry hadn't described the target exactly. He said it would be easy to see. On a real mission, we'd know precisely what it looked like. But Henry liked to test us when we were training.

"Got it," said Maria, and then I saw it too.

There was a large X marked out on the ground. I laughed. What a cliché. Henry must have wanted to make it easy for us on our first live run.

There was no more time to muse. I focused on what I had to do, with my finger poised over the bomb release.

"Now," said Maria, just before we passed over the X.

"Bombs away," I said, keeping level and increasing the throttle a little to get clear after the bombs were dropped. The seconds ticked by and then there was a tremendous explosion behind us as the bombs went off.

"Christ!" said Maria, turning around to look. "Now that's a firework."

We were well past the target and out of danger. I went around in a wide arc to watch the next plane coming in. Smoke was billowing from the target zone. The next team dropped their bomb almost dead on top of where ours had been and continued just as we had. It was easier when you already had smoke to mark the area. Seconds later their bombs exploded.

This time we got to see it properly. It was quite a sight. I kept circling, joined by the other planes. Normally we would have flown away from the target zone to a rendezvous point, but this was still practice.

Within a short space of time, four more planes unloaded their ordnance without a hitch. The smoke billowing out from each successive blast probably made it more difficult for the succeeding pilots, but they carried on regardless. This was the job and it was being carried out with great efficiency.

It was going extremely well and I was just about to say so when Maria said, "Linda is too close."

I looked across at Linda's Mosquito and saw that Maria was right. Her kite was nearer to the plane in front than the others had been.

"Bluebird Seven," I said. "Pull back a little. You're too close."

There was no response.

"Bluebird Seven," I repeated. "Pull back."

The plane in front dropped its bombs and flew on.

"Bluebird Seven, do you read me?" I said, more urgently.

But it was too late. I watched in horror as Linda's plane flew into the bomb blast. Her plane pitched up violently and she banked out of her line, almost clipping the ground. I could see that the prop on the starboard engine had stopped working; it was spinning slowly, no longer under power. Linda was fighting for control of the plane while in the background the bombing run continued.

My heart was in my mouth as I watched her plane dive towards the ground and then somehow recover. I knew the Mosquito could fly on one engine, but was Linda going to be able to retain control?

"She's got it, I think," said Maria as we circled around again, watching Linda struggle. I imagined her wrestling with the controls, fighting to get the plane level.

Surprisingly there was no word from Henry. He must have seen it. I realised he was leaving it to me as Flight Leader. This was now my problem.

In the meantime, the last of the flight dropped their bombs and sped away from the now smoking and cratered target zone. I couldn't wait for Linda; I had to get everyone in order and hope she would make it.

"Bluebirds," I said. "Form up on me, close formation."

The others joined me in their familiar positions. We were taking one more pass around the target zone. Since this was a practice, I felt justified in doing so. To my immense relief, Linda seemed to finally get the better of her plane.

"She's got it," said Maria.

"Thank goodness for that," I replied.

Sure enough, the Mosquito was in level flight. There was nothing for it now but to leave Linda to make her own way home.

"Bluebird Seven, get back to base as best you can," I said. "Bluebirds on me, we're going back low-level."

"Wilco," said Linda, finally answering me.

There were going to be some questions when she got back to Hawberry. Why hadn't she responded? I took the flight down low once more and headed for the airfield once Maria gave us the bearing.

On a real mission, we would have had to rendezvous and get out regardless. If this happened to one of the flight, then they would be on their own to try and make it back to Blighty. I sincerely hoped Linda would make it back all right.

It was a small hop to Hawberry. We approached the runway in short order and landed. I taxied to our standing and killed the engine.

"What now?" said Maria.

"We wait for Linda and debrief," I said. "Find out why the hell she didn't answer."

"Now you really *are* sounding like a leader."

We jumped down from the Mosquito and waited for Linda's kite to appear. It would be much slower on one engine.

Connie lit up a cigarette and took a puff, then she passed it to Jennifer. "What the hell happened?" she said.

"She was too close to the blast, that's what happened," said Susan.

"We were right behind her, and we saw her get hit," added Pamela.

"I hope she makes it back," said Shelly.

Right on cue, the drone of a Mosquito split the air. In the distance, I could see Linda's plane with Henry's Spitfire following it in.

"Here she comes," said Susan.

Though the Mosquito was flying on one engine, it made a perfect landing. We watched it taxi over to the hangars and come to a stop.

"She's a good pilot," Susan observed.

"She's a lucky pilot," said Patricia.

After turning off the one remaining engine, Linda and ASO Janice Kipling, her navigator, walked over to us. I went forward to meet them. Maria came with me.

"That was hairy," said Linda as she reached us.

"Didn't you hear me tell you to pull back?" I asked her.

Linda hesitated.

"You were too close," added Maria. "Anna told you to pull back."

"I thought it was fine," said Linda defensively.

It wasn't a good response. It didn't address the issue, or rather, it did. She had simply ignored me. I knew I could not let it go.

"You could have been killed," I said. "Both of you."

"I know, I realise that now," said Linda.

Maria glanced at me. I knew I had to say something. I took a breath.

"I'm the Flight Leader," I said bluntly. "If I tell you to pull back, then you bloody well pull back."

Linda hesitated. Henry was watching us keenly from a distance; perhaps she was aware of that. She backed down. "I'm sorry. You're right," she said at last.

"And answer your damn radio next time," I continued, now my blood was up.

"Yes, I will."

"We can't afford to have that happen on a mission," I said. "On a mission, you might not come back. I don't want that. It's my job to bring the flight back intact and all of you alive."

Linda looked at me and nodded.

"Maybe you should go and see to your plane," I suggested. "See if it's reparable."

"Sure."

Linda and Janice turned away and walked back to the hangars, talking in low voices. Maria smiled at me triumphantly. "Well done," she said. "That's the spirit."

"I think I need some spirits," I said with a sigh, and Maria laughed.

"You're a damn good leader, and don't you forget it," she said quietly.

A movement caught my eye over by Linda's Mosquito. I squinted and put my hand up to shade my eyes. "Is that Gary?" I asked Maria.

"Where?"

"Over there."

She peered in the direction I indicated. "Yes, it is Gary. What on earth is he still doing on the base?"

"I don't know, but I mean to find out," I said grimly. But before I could, Henry came up to us.

"You did well," he said.

"Thank you, sir," I replied.

"Sometimes you need to assert your leadership," he told me. "It's part of the job."

"I know," I said. "I'm just not used to having to do it."

"Then get used to it," he replied in an uncompromising tone. "Anyway, get back to the Hall for a debrief. I'll go and see whether they can repair that plane."

"Yes, sir."

I saluted as he turned on his heel and walked away. We rejoined the others.

"What was all that about with Linda?" asked Shelly as we all walked to the truck.

"Our Flight Leader was just asserting her authority," said Maria.

"Linda thinks she should have been Flight Leader," Connie said. "That's what I've heard."

"Well," said Jennifer, "she's not, so she can dream on. We've got the Flight Leader we need."

I was a little shocked to discover that there was some rivalry on the team, or that anyone resented my position.

"Look," I cut in, "we're a team, we're in this together. Let's focus on that."

"Yes, that's true," said Jennifer. "But we've got your back, Anna, don't you worry. If anyone questions your right to lead this flight, we're right behind you."

When we arrived at the Hall, I left the others and sought out James. He was in his office at his desk. He looked up and smiled when I entered.

"Anna," he said. "What can I do for you?"

Instead of exchanging pleasantries, I launched right into it. "Why is Gary over at the hangars, wearing overalls, sir?" I asked him.

"Ah," he said. "Why don't you sit down, instead of looming over me?"

His manner was disarming and also distracting. I tried to hold onto my irritation about Gary, but it immediately deserted me. I sat down in the chair opposite him.

"We made him a mechanic. We didn't know what else to do with him," he said, almost apologetically.

"What?"

"I know it's rather unorthodox," said James. "But he was thoroughly questioned by our friends from MI6 and he's definitely not a spy. He really is a reporter."

"Then why didn't you let him go back to reporting?" I asked.

"For one thing, he didn't want to, and for another … we couldn't."

"Couldn't?"

James sighed. "We had to make him sign the Official Secrets Act. We were dubious about him sticking to it, even so. Then he confessed that he didn't really want to be a reporter. It turns out that he's got a fair bit of experience as a car mechanic, and well … we thought he might be useful."

"I see," was all I could manage to say.

"You don't approve?" he asked.

"It's not for me to approve or not, sir," I told him.

"You can say what you really think; don't mind me."

"I don't know what to think," I admitted. "And I suppose you're right, what could you do with him anyway?"

"We'll wait and see how he works out. If he doesn't, well, we can always go back to your original solution."

I must have looked shocked, because he suddenly laughed.

"I'm joking. We're not going to throw anyone out of a plane," he said, a smile playing on his lips. My heart did one of those annoying flips.

"Thank goodness for that," I murmured.

"Anyway, how did it go today?" he asked, changing the subject.

"All right for the most part," I replied. I ran through what had happened with Linda's plane and the subsequent conversation with her. He listened without comment.

"Unfortunately, these things happen," he said. "Timing is critical. It sounds like you handled it well enough."

It was an indication of his confidence in me that he said nothing further. A thought surfaced which had been bothering me for a while, and it seemed as good a time as any to ask. "What happens if one of our team is killed on a mission?"

"It would be unfortunate," he replied.

"Yes, of course, but we'd be one plane short and we've no replacements. How long would it take to train another team, or even two?"

He sighed a little more heavily this time and leaned back in his chair. He knew exactly what I was getting at. "You're right, of course. I've pointed this out to the powers that be more than once."

"And?"

"And this is all they'll give me until we've proven ourselves on a mission … or rather *you've* proven yourselves."

The import of this sunk in. "So, if our first mission fails, we're destined for the scrapheap, is that what you're saying?" I asked.

"Not the scrapheap, no, but probably the ATA to transport planes like the others…"

He meant like the other female pilots, of course. But I didn't want to transport planes, not anymore. Vistas had opened up which I had never dreamed of. As much as I feared the prospect of our first mission, I relished the excitement. I'd flown in the face of danger in my little Tiger Moth, but this was different. This was life or death. This was war.

"I have allies and I have detractors," James said by way of explanation. "It's up to us to turn the detractors into allies."

"So, we're just an experiment to some people, is that it?" I said, feeling a little miffed and at the same time determined not to fail.

"That's not how I view it. I didn't start this enterprise with any expectation other than success."

I had heard enough. I stood up, filled with a new resolve. "All right," I said. "Then I'm going to make damn sure the first mission goes swimmingly."

"That's the spirit." He hesitated, then continued, "I'm probably not supposed to tell you this right now, but you've earned the right to know. You're going to get the chance far sooner than you think."

So, the first mission was imminent. "We won't let you down, sir," I told him.

"I know, I'm counting on it."

After lunch, there was a debrief about the mission. James, Henry and Gloria stood on the podium as usual in the briefing room.

"I'm not going to say much about what happened this morning," said James. "Suffice it to say that timing is everything. A second or two can make all the difference between life and death." He paused and it seemed he was looking directly at Linda. She pretended to be studying the ceiling. "Good communication is vital on a mission. There are very few second chances if you make a mistake. Today's exercise will be repeated, followed by strafing practice at ground targets. You will then have a spell of night navigation."

Henry spoke next. "The technical crew informs me the damage to the Mosquito engine from the bomb blast was not too serious," he said. "But it might take a day or two to repair."

"While that's happening, you'll be glad to know you won't be idle," put in Gloria. "You can attend further classes and drill."

There were groans all around.

"I'd be perfectly fine being idle," Shelly whispered.

Maria suppressed a laugh.

CHAPTER TEN

A day later Linda's plane was once more ready to fly. Speculation was rife regarding the impending mission as we headed for the planes in one of the trucks.

"I think it's going to be a night mission," said Connie, tapping the ash off her cigarette over the back of the truck.

"That would be fun," said Maria, sarcastically. "Flying at low level in the bloody dark…"

She wasn't wrong; it was hairy enough in daylight. How the hell were we supposed to see anything at night?

"It's obviously a ground attack involving strafing and bombing," said Pamela.

"Perhaps we should just focus on the job and worry about the mission when we're told what it is," I put in.

"A real mission … where we could die…" said Shelly all of a sudden.

"For goodness' sake, don't be so morbid, Shelly," said Patricia.

"But it's true," said Shelly defensively.

"As if we needed bloody well reminding," said Connie, passing the rest of her cigarette to Jennifer, who took a long drag on it.

"Nobody's going to die," I told them. "Not on my watch."

"You see," said Maria, glaring at Shelly. "That's the kind of talk we need. We're all going to do our best to come back alive."

The truck fell silent. Nobody wanted to contradict me, but the reality was I couldn't be sure. For a start, I'd never even been in combat.

The truck came to a stop and we piled out, ready to face another practice session.

Over the next few days, we practised bombing runs in ones, twos and threes, leaving several craters on the local gunnery range. Then we practised strafing wooden targets in the shape of planes. We fired our cannons, coming in low and then dropping ordnance. Finally, we undertook night-flying practice.

"You'll be relying on your compass headings, timings and easily recognisable landmarks," Henry told us. "That means you have to know the route far better than you think. Study the maps and reconnaissance photos carefully. You'll need to fly a little higher than in the daytime to keep above potential obstacles like telegraph poles. Go lower only if and when you are certain. Keep your eyes on what's in front of you."

As I fired up the Mosquito for the first run, I was thankful that at least the runway was lit up.

"Here goes nothing," I said to Maria as I wound up the engines for take-off.

"I've got you," she replied. "Never fear."

I flicked her a grateful glance. We had become a team, exactly as James had hoped. I wondered if it was the same for the others and thought it probably was.

"Bluebird Leader, you're clear," said Control.

We barrelled down the runway and the wheels left the ground. I kept a careful check on the altimeter as I circled around, waiting for the others. We kept our navigation lights on so that we could at least see the planes on either side. Over enemy territory, we would turn them off. Navigation had to be done by dead reckoning using the compass, waypoints and landmarks. It was taxing, even for excellent navigators like Maria.

The rest of the flight joined us, checking in as they did so. "Bluebird Two on station… Bluebird Three on station…" came the calls one by one.

"Bluebirds, close formation, low level, on me," I said, dropping down as far as I dared. The monochrome landscape came sharply into focus as I opened up the throttle.

"Bearing two oh seven," said Maria, giving the compass heading, and then we were off.

Flying at night was completely different. Details I could see in the day were lacking; instead, there were shadows, patches of light and dark. I had to keep up the speed while straining to see what was in front of me.

Maria kept half an eye on the terrain while she studied the map. I dropped low over open fields and then higher over the woods. Even so, I was worried about hitting telegraph lines or some other unforeseen obstacle.

"Christ, that was close," said Maria as we zoomed up and over a farmhouse.

"Sorry…"

"It's all right. One more heart attack and I'm a goner, that's all," she quipped.

I laughed and banked as she gave us a new bearing.

Fields, hedges, roads and stretches of water glistening in the moonlight — all were now hazards. My vision began to adjust and I felt emboldened to open up the throttle and go a little lower.

"Easy," said Maria.

We were streaking low across a field when we both spotted a telegraph line coming up at speed.

"Lines!" shouted Maria.

I pulled up hard on the throttle and the Mosquito rapidly gained height. My heart was thumping and my hand was frozen on the stick.

"Level off," she said.

"What? Oh…" I said, realising we'd gone too high.

"I'd prefer not to do die today," quipped Maria.

"Sorry… I lost it for a moment…" I felt a little embarrassed.

"Bluebird Leader, are we meant to be this high?" It was Jennifer.

"No, I'm taking us down," I replied.

"Roger."

As I pushed the stick forward to resume a more sensible height, another voice came over the radio.

"Planes at three o'clock coming in fast." It was Patricia.

"Are they bandits, Blue Two?" I asked her while looking over to our right to see for myself. Sure enough, three shadows were winging their way towards us.

"Negative, they're running lights, they look like ours… Hurricanes probably," Patricia replied.

I breathed a sigh of relief. The last thing we needed was to come under attack in the dark.

"Bluebirds stay on course," I said.

The three planes flew over the top of us, no doubt to check us out. Their profile silhouetted in the moonlight indicated they were indeed Hurricanes. They didn't attempt to make contact, but I radioed it in, nevertheless.

"Control, we've been intercepted by a friendly patrol."

"Roger, Bluebird Leader, we're aware. Carry on," came the response.

"Wilco, Control," I said.

Control would have picked up the communication that we'd been spotted and dealt with it appropriately. There was no doubt a cover story for our squadron.

"Relax," said Maria, noting my tension.

I flicked her a grateful glance. "Where would I be without you?"

"In a ditch somewhere, I imagine," she retorted with a smile. "Here's the next bearing. Let's get to it."

I took the kite back down to a low level, mile after mile taking all my attention. I felt mentally exhausted by the time the runway lights at Hawberry came into view.

The wheels touched down and I taxied the kite to the standings. I looked at my watch as we jumped down from the plane — it was midnight.

We walked to the truck with the others.

"What was all that about, sis?" Jennifer asked me.

"I was slightly fazed for a moment," I replied.

"The telegraph lines jumped out of nowhere and she got spooked," put in Maria.

Everyone laughed.

"The night flying was pretty scary," said Patricia.

"You'll get used to it," Susan assured her.

"You've flown at night before?" I asked her.

"Yes, transporting planes, but usually at a much higher altitude."

"When those Hurricanes buzzed us, I thought it was Jerry for a moment," said Pamela.

She had not been the only one. We all knew we were bound to encounter friendly planes from time to time. We just had to keep quiet on the radio when it happened. Our planes had RAF decals and markings, which should be sufficient to identify us. Control would deal with the protocols.

"Right now, I'm too tired to think about anything except sleep," said Connie as we climbed into the back of the truck.

"How many more of these night flights have we got to do?" asked Jennifer, yawning and laying her head on Connie's shoulder.

"As many as it takes," said Maria, ever practical.

Connie lit up a cigarette and smoked it while looking out of the truck. She and Jennifer seemed to have become quite close. I experienced a slight pang, because Jennifer and I had always been close. I gave myself a mental shake. Friendships were bound to form in a situation like this.

"I heard Linda talking to some of the others," said Pamela.

"And?" said Susan.

"She was saying that experience should count for something…"

"Not this again!" Maria fired up.

"I'm sure she didn't mean anything by it," said Susan, trying to placate her.

"It's not just experience that makes for a good Flight Leader," said Maria, determined to defend me. "There are other qualities which Anna has — plus she's a bloody good pilot."

I listened quietly as the argument continued, not wanting to intervene. I couldn't fathom why Linda would covet my position. It wasn't an easy role, as I was discovering as time went on. However, I wasn't about to give it up either.

CHAPTER ELEVEN

Over the following week we flew night practice after night practice. It was unrelenting. The only upside was that we were allowed to sleep in and have a late-morning start. I began to notice there was an air of anticipation around the place, as if something was in the offing.

We were assembled once more in the briefing room as James, Henry, Gloria and the Marx Brothers took to the podium.

"Aye, aye," whispered Shelly, eyeing the two spies. "Something going on."

We were told things on a need-to-know basis. Due to the secret nature of the unit, those in charge played their cards very close to their chests.

James stepped forward to speak and the room fell silent.

"Not long ago, I intimated that the skills you have so diligently been learning would be put into practice for real." He paused. "That day has now arrived."

Shelly shot me a triumphant look. I had mixed feelings. Although part of me had longed for this moment, now it was here I knew it meant that some of us may not survive it.

"This mission," James continued, "is a significant milestone for us all, as well as having a great deal of strategic value. I will now hand over to our MI6 colleagues, who will explain the operation in more detail."

The Marx Brothers got to their feet and stepped forward.

"Operation Hornet," said Harpo, "will take place in two days' time."

"The target," said Chico, indicating the large map on the wall behind them, "will be the airfield of Caen-Carpiquet, about three miles west of Caen itself. It is of strategic importance because it's used for fighter-bomber operations across the Channel. We intend to neutralise their operations by means of a low-level bombing and strafing strike on the airfield, rendering the runway unusable and destroying as many planes and buildings as possible."

"This mission is doubly important to the Sirens," said Harpo. "Not only will it prove what you are capable of, but it will also reinforce the ability of Mosquitos in precision strike operations."

The two of them took long drags on their cigarettes, almost in unison, to allow their words to sink in.

"It will lay to rest once and for all the question of whether women can successfully engage in operational combat missions," added James with a sudden fervour. "Which, as you know, is a cause we have all been fighting for. You're going to show those in command that these weren't just empty words. Am I right?"

As one body, we stood up and cheered, stamping our feet. It was a release of tension, knowing that all the training hadn't been for nothing; that we were about to make a real difference in the war. James, the Marx Brothers, Henry and Gloria smiled at our reaction. They waited until we had settled down.

"All right," said Harpo. "We will go over this in more detail, but for now we'll give you a summary of the operation."

"The mission is scheduled to take place in three days' time," said Chico. "The Sirens will take off in the early hours of the morning. The raid will be timed to take place as dawn is breaking. That way, you won't be flying over enemy territory in the dark, and will hopefully catch the Jerries napping."

A ripple of laughter accompanied this quip.

"You will fly the mission at a low level in order to avoid radar detection by the Germans. We don't want Jerry to know you are coming, obviously," put in Harpo.

"You will fly directly to the target," continued Chico. "It consists of an eighteen-hundred-yard runway, an ammo dump in the landing area, several hangars and a control tower. Based on reconnaissance photos, we expect at least one squadron of Focke-Wulf fighter aircraft to be stationed there. Your job is to destroy as much of that as possible and all of the planes if you can."

"There are a number of flak positions," said Harpo. "But we expect you to be in and out again before they can be properly deployed."

Now that the target and the main purpose of the mission had been revealed, Henry stepped forward. "I will be the Mission I/C," he said. He pointed to someone at the back of the room, and I turned to see that a projector had been set up.

The lights were dimmed as Gloria pulled a projection screen down over the map. A reconnaissance photo of the airfield appeared on the screen. Henry took a long pointer and indicated a spot on the photograph.

"You will approach from the northwest of the airfield in two teams of six planes each, Alpha and Beta. Alpha will drop ordnance along the runway before turning back and strafing the planes which, as you can see —" he moved the pointer — "are lined up here. Simultaneously, Beta will fly across the buildings, dropping ordnance to destroy as many of those as they can. Beta will then return to carry out a strafing run alongside Alpha. Having done that, you will all get the hell out of there as fast as you possibly can."

There was silence as we absorbed this. This was no longer a drill, a practice run, this was the real deal.

"We will go over this in detail over the next two days to ensure that you all understand the mission objectives and how to carry them out. I will be issuing a flight plan which has been worked out, including the flight path and timings. You are not to deviate from this plan. Are there any questions?"

A hand went up. "Yes, ASO Hartley?"

"Sir, what if we are intercepted?"

"We are not anticipating that," said Henry. "But were it to happen, then you'd turn and run back to Blighty as fast as you were able. We'd work out what happened and go again with a new plan." He paused in case there were any more questions. When were none, he continued, "You need to study the reconnaissance photos carefully and go over the plans for the bombing runs. Try and imprint the target area on your minds. There are photographs of the route you're taking, so you can be aware of any hazards and so forth. We are trying to give you the best chance of success."

James stepped forward again. "Until the mission is over, nobody is to leave the base for any reason," he said. "It goes without saying that complete secrecy is required. The details of this mission and the target are only known to you and to anyone carrying out operational support. Do not discuss it outside of your circle, is that clear?"

There was a murmur, which apparently wasn't good enough for James.

"I said, is that *clear*?" he said a little louder and more forcefully.

"Yes, sir," came the chorus in response.

"All right, take a thirty-minute break and then we'll get into the nuts and bolts of the operation."

As we dispersed for a cup of tea and biscuits, there was a fair bit of chatter. When we entered the dining room, though, all talk about the mission ceased. There were other personnel in the room, and we needed to heed what James had said.

Our usual group sat together at a table well away from anyone else and spoke in hushed tones.

"Who do you think will be leading the Alpha and Beta teams?" asked Shelly at once.

"Anna will lead one of them, obviously," said Maria.

"And the other?" Connie said, taking a sip of her tea.

"I hope it's not Linda," said Jennifer.

"Whoever it is," I said, "will be the person they think is best for the job."

After the short break, the more detailed briefings began. Just before lunch, Judy, James's adjutant, appeared by my side.

"Wing Commander Donnington wishes to see you, ma'am," she said.

There was a chorus of 'oohs' from the others and I tried to shush them. "Stop it, you lot," I told them crossly, but they just laughed.

I followed Judy along various corridors and ended up in a small salon I had not seen before. It sported blue furniture and ornate mouldings on the walls and ceiling. It was furnished with easy chairs and sofas, as well as a table at one end where James was sitting. The table had place settings for two.

He got up as Judy ushered me in. "Anna," he said. "Thanks for coming."

"I assumed it was an order," I replied a little formally, but his smile disarmed me.

"I just wanted to talk to you about something important," he said. "So, I arranged for us to have lunch; I hope you don't mind?"

The sideboard held some silver containers with candles underneath to keep them warm.

"Not at all," I said, chiding myself for sounding unappreciative.

"Help yourself to some food and have a seat," he said, indicating the sideboard.

I picked up a plate and opened the containers, revealing slices of gammon, potatoes in parsley butter and some green vegetables. I took a good portion, since we didn't get gammon all that often. There was also some gravy. I sat down opposite James, who also had a full plate.

"You could have just met me in your office," I observed, taking a mouthful of food.

"Where's the fun in that?" he replied. His eyes twinkled and I tried not to be distracted by them.

"Do you eat up here often?" I asked with interest.

"Only when the top brass come to visit," he said with a laugh. "Today I thought I'd make an exception. Privileges of rank."

"I'm honoured," I said.

"You're doing a fantastic job, Anna. I just wanted you to know that."

"Not everyone thinks so," I blurted out and then flushed.

It had become apparent that at least one person resented my position, which stung a little.

"That's inevitable," James replied. "But experience isn't everything. You have the qualities of leadership that we're looking for, as I've told you before."

I decided he must know about Linda, but was being diplomatic. I wasn't surprised. He seemed to know a great deal about what went on around the base.

"Thanks," I said. "I'm doing my best." I wasn't used to receiving such high praise.

"I wanted to talk to you about the two teams, Alpha and Beta. You'll lead one of them, naturally, and you will be the overall Flight Leader for the mission. It's just during the attack that we need to split the flight. Which team would you like to lead?" he said.

I took another forkful of food while I thought about his question. Which target would I like to take on? Did it really matter? He waited for me to make a choice.

"I'll lead Alpha," I said. I liked the idea of strafing the planes as much as anything.

"Good choice," he replied. "Now pick the rest of your team."

That was easy. "SO Jennifer Nightingale, SO Patricia Batley, SO Susan Bell, SO Virginia Goodman and SO Carol Davies," I told him. I didn't know Virginia or Carol so well, but they were good pilots.

"All right," said James. "Although I was considering Jennifer to lead Beta."

"I want her with me," I replied at once. I couldn't help the instinct to protect my sister.

"I understand," he said without further comment. "Who would you pick to lead Beta, then?"

I didn't have to think about that; there was one obvious choice. "SO Linda Harris," I said.

James looked at me keenly but didn't question my decision. We both knew I was trying to mollify Linda just a little.

"That's settled then," he said. "I will announce the two teams after lunch."

We ate in silence until James said, "Tell me a little bit about yourself, if you will?"

I was surprised by the personal question. "What do you want to know?"

"Your life before you came here, what was it like?"

"Well, I'm a farm girl at heart…" I began.

We conversed while we finished the main course. Then we had dessert — a slice of apple pie — followed by a cup of tea. To be fair, I did most of the talking. James was a good listener and sat in amused silence while I told him my life story.

"I'm glad to know you better," he said when I came to the end.

"But I don't really know *you*," I pointed out. I thought he might share something of himself with me, but I was destined to be disappointed.

"Perhaps another time," he said, looking at his watch. "We've got a briefing to attend."

"Oh, yes, sorry." I shot him a guilty look.

"Don't apologise," he said. "It was a pleasant way to pass the time. Sometimes it's good to take a breather, don't you think?"

"Yes," I said, flustered by his sudden formality. So, I was just someone to pass the time with?

"I'll see myself out," I said, walking quickly to the door.

"Absolutely," he replied, watching me go. "See you shortly."

I made my way back to the others with my mind awhirl. I was angry that I had read too much into the invitation to dine with James and his subsequent interest in my life.

"Where have you been?" asked Maria when I joined the group.

"Lunch with James, that's all," I replied.

"Ooh," said Shelly.

"It was just business," I said, still bristling.

"Just business … sure," said Connie in disbelieving tones.

Looks were exchanged but Jennifer stepped in. "Come on, let's get to the briefing."

During the briefing, the two attack teams were announced and who would be leading them. We would rehearse the precise attack manoeuvres the following morning. This was crucial to the success of the mission and to ensure that none of our planes were hit by the blowback when dropping ordnance.

As we finished for the afternoon, Linda came up to me.

"Was it your idea to make me Beta Leader?" she asked without preamble.

"Well, I —" I began.

"I thought so," she said, cutting me off. "I don't need your charity, Nightingale. When I become Flight Leader, I expect to earn it."

"It wasn't charity," I said, but Linda had already turned on her heel and walked away. The others approached.

"Bloody cheek!" Maria raged. I noticed that her fists were clenched.

"Leave it, Maria, please," I said. "We can't afford to fight amongst ourselves. There's a mission to fly, remember? I don't need you to be court-martialled for hitting a fellow officer, I need you as my navigator, and so do the Sirens."

Maria sighed and relaxed her fists.

"*Did* you pick Linda to lead Beta?" Patricia asked me.

"Yes, I did… I thought…"

"There's no pleasing some people," observed Connie.

"Just let her try anything, that's all I'm saying," said Maria.

"Easy, tiger," said Shelly, laughing.

"Look," said Pamela, "I don't know about the rest of you, but I want my supper. Some of us didn't get a personal lunch invitation and I'm famished."

Even I laughed at this. I put Linda firmly from my mind and headed for the dining room.

Later that night as we lay in bed, Jennifer quizzed me on my lunch with James.

"You're sweet on him, aren't you?" she said quietly once I had finished telling her.

"Jenny, he's the CO. If we — you know, started something, then people like Linda would think I got to where I am just because of that."

"Who cares what they think?" she said, dismissing my objections.

"I do," I said. "And anyway, I don't even know what he thinks of me. I don't even know if he wants to start something."

"You could simply ask him," she suggested.

I turned away from her. "No, Jenny, I can't. I would never be able to look at him again."

"Then you'll just have to wait and see if he makes a move, dear sister," she said prosaically and hugged me tight.

"What if he doesn't?" I whispered.

"Well, then you'll know, won't you?"

I didn't answer her. I knew I needed to focus on the mission. Everything else would have to wait, or perhaps matters would simply resolve themselves in time. It was something my father always used to tell me when I was worried. I hoped very much that he was right.

CHAPTER TWELVE

The night before the mission arrived all too soon. James held a pre-mission briefing along with Henry, Gloria and the Marx Brothers as usual. We would be leaving in the early hours of the morning. This was the last chance for some final words from them.

The Marx Brothers spoke first. Harpo stood up, cigarette in hand.

"First, I just want to say how proud we are of the Sirens and what you have achieved even to get to this point. We have every confidence in your success. There are just a couple of rather important things we've left until this point to tell you."

Chico joined him and took a drag on his cigarette. "You will each be issued with two grenades," he said, "as well as sidearms. The grenades are not standard issue to pilots but in your case, if you are shot down and unable to return, then these can be used to destroy the aircraft."

I glanced at the faces around me; they were steadfast. We'd had training using grenades and now we knew why. We also knew that destroying the aircraft meant pulling the pin with you inside it; Chico didn't have to say it.

"In addition," said Harpo, "you will each be issued with a packet containing a pill. That pill is for use if you get captured. It contains cyanide. It's a quick death, so I'm told… Make sure you keep them handy."

The hard reality of the mission hit me then. I resolved to make it home.

"We don't need to tell you how essential it is to keep the Sirens a secret from the Germans," said Chico. "But we want you to come back, so do your damnedest to make sure that you do."

They sat down and Henry stepped forward.

"I want to wish you good luck and Godspeed. You're some of the best pilots and navigators we've trained. I'm sorry that more people won't get to know it, but I know that you will do your duty and carry out this mission successfully. Thank you."

James gestured to Gloria.

"I second everything Henry has just said. I couldn't have said it better. I'll look forward to seeing you back here after the mission," she said.

James nodded in approval. He would have the final words. "I'm damn proud of you all," he said, looking around the room. I heard the passion in his voice. He paused for a moment, then suddenly he became quite poetic. "Never forget who you are: you are the Sirens, flying like shadows across the landscape. Your exploits will never be known, but you will be heroes just the same. There will be no medals, no Victoria Cross, no accolades, but you will have the satisfaction of knowing you have played a key role in the war effort. There will be people — very few people — high up in the ranks, in government, who'll know your secret and will be grateful for your service. *We* are grateful for your service. Thank you. Now get some sleep."

As he left the podium, the Sirens stood up and cheered at his rousing words. I watched him go and wished he'd said goodbye to me.

"Come on," I said, turning to my friends and colleagues. "Let's get to bed — we have an early start tomorrow."

We repaired to our rooms, or at least I did. Jennifer wasn't with me. I wondered where she might be. By chance I looked out of the window onto the formal gardens beyond. A movement caught my eye in the moonlight. As I peered through the glass, I made out Jennifer and Connie walking together arm in arm, sharing a cigarette and smiling. There was a tenderness between them.

I pulled back from the window and put my mind back on the mission. My flying gear was laid out on a chair along with Jennifer's, ready for the morning. I set the alarm and got into bed. As I was falling asleep, Jennifer slipped quietly into the room. A few moments later, she slid under the covers and pulled in close. It was comforting.

"Jenny," I murmured. "You and Connie seem to be getting quite close."

"Yes," she said. "We are."

"Be careful…"

"I'm always careful."

I let it go; we had a mission to fly. Besides, none of us knew if we'd see each other again after tomorrow.

"Anna," she said softly, as if reading my thoughts. "You're not allowed to die."

I turned to face her, suddenly awake. "Neither are you," I said.

"Promise me you won't," she said.

"Can *you* promise me that?" I asked her, knowing neither of us could.

"Well, then we'll do our best to come back," she said. "How about that?"

"All right." I smiled. "Now let's get some sleep."

All too soon, the alarm broke into my fitful slumber. I sat up, wide awake.

"What time is it?" asked Jennifer sleepily.

"Time to go," I said.

We performed our ablutions and put on our flying gear. As we were doing so, there was a soft knock on the door. I opened it to find Maria and Shelly.

"Just checking you hadn't overslept," Maria said.

"We're ready," I replied. "Let's go."

As we walked down the silent corridors we were joined by the others. Nobody spoke as we stepped outside into the brisk early morning air. It was still dark and I was glad we were wearing warm clothing. We piled into the trucks. As always Connie sat at the back with Jennifer, sharing a last cigarette.

I thought of my parents and how they would feel if Jennifer or I died. What could we tell them? Not the truth. They would be devastated, just as families all over the country were shocked every day at the news of the loss of a loved one to the war. The war, which had seemed so remote to me, was now here, and we were about to be in the thick of it.

The trucks pulled up at the airfield and we jumped out. We stood in a group, and then I realised that everyone was waiting for me.

"Everyone got their grenades and their pill?" I said, pulling myself together. I patted my breast pocket, where I had put my cyanide capsule.

There were murmurs of assent.

"All right then," I said, looking at my watch. "Take-off in fifteen minutes. Let's get this done and make sure we all come back."

Maria and I climbed up into the Mosquito and strapped in.

"Not much point in these parachutes if we can't bail out," said Maria, closing the hatch.

"We can bail in the Channel or over Blighty," I said. "Of course we need them."

She laughed. "I never thought of that."

"We're not going to need those pills," I said. "Or the grenades. Because we are coming back, come hell or high water."

"That's the spirit," said Maria.

I fired up the engines and flicked on the navigation lights. We went rapidly through the preflight checks. Maria looked over her route one more time and then I got the flight to check in.

"Wildcats, are you ready?"

Wildcats was our codename for the mission. It felt appropriate. The answers came back promptly.

"Wildcat One ready."

"Wildcat Two ready."

Once we reached eleven, I radioed Control.

"Control, this is Wildcat Leader requesting clearance to take off," I said.

"Wildcat Leader, you're clear. Godspeed."

"Roger, see you later, Control," I replied, easing up the throttle and taxiing to the end of the runway, followed by eleven other Mosquitos.

"This is it," I said to Maria.

"It certainly is," she replied, looking at her watch. "Now."

I opened up the throttle and we sped up the runway. In moments we were airborne. I circled above the airbase, waiting for the others to join me, which they did in short order.

Maria gave them the heading.

"Close formation," I said. "On me. Keep it low and keep it tight all the way to the Big Show."

Big Show was the codename for the target. I dropped the Mosquito down low and opened up the throttle. The kite responded beautifully. Perhaps my senses were heightened by the prospect of combat, but it felt as if it was ready for action.

"This wasn't what I expected for my first visit to France," quipped Maria.

"Me neither."

Then I had to focus as the ground flashed by beneath us. The route south was one we'd flown several times during training. The adrenaline was already flowing, putting me on high alert.

Maria was watching her compass, reading the map and keeping a weather eye on the terrain up ahead. The familiar routine kicked in.

"Trees."

"Got it."

"Lines."

"Seen them."

As we neared the coast, I saw the South Downs shrouded in mist. Something we hadn't thought of, but predictable for an early winter's morning.

"Damn," I said, taking us higher. I couldn't risk hitting something in the mist. "Let's hope the German radar doesn't spot us," I said as we gained height.

Fortunately, the mist wasn't more than twenty or thirty feet off the ground. It was a strangely eerie sight as trees, poles and the tops of houses poked out of it.

The tension in the cockpit was palpable as we neared the coastline. Once we left the shores of Blighty, we would become a target. The mist cleared and we dropped down over Chichester Harbour, heading for West Wittering.

"Wildcats, kill the lights," I said, turning off our navigation lights. "Radio silence."

One by one the navigation lights were extinguished and the planes around us became black hulks. We had to keep radio comms to a minimum because we were told the Germans would be actively listening, and we didn't want to give them any time to try and zero in on us.

"Here's the Channel," said Maria as we crossed over onto the water.

"This is it," I replied, knowing we were now leaving friendly airspace. From here on in, anything could happen.

"Wildcats, keep them peeled," I said as Maria gave them the bearing. Then there really was silence apart from the hum of the engines. I took us low over the Channel, which was quite calm with small waves. We had to cross that expanse of black water in the dark.

I kept a weather eye out for shipping; at this height we could easily slam into the side of a destroyer or merchant vessel. As luck would have it, there was nothing for us to avoid. It was a straight run. Eventually, the French coastline came into view and the grey light of predawn began to appear on the horizon. Our timing was spot on.

We flew over the beach and made landfall near Mont Fleury, to avoid any coastal batteries. If there were lookouts, we'd be over and past before they realised we were there. That was the hope, anyway.

"So far so good," said Maria as the French landscape spread out before us. At any other time it would have looked magnificent. Now it was uninviting, an enemy landscape, and we were the intruders.

The route took us across the least populated areas, avoiding towns and keeping low all the way. I'd tried to memorise the photographs, looking out for potential hazards. We had to rely on our eyes and senses.

Huge swathes of open agricultural land helped us make good time. Hedges and clumps of trees cut across our path. We hopped up and over, just as we had practised. We'd been flying for the best part of an hour. It was the longest we'd flown one way, but I knew I couldn't lose concentration. Besides, there was still the trip back to think about.

"Okay?" asked Maria, flicking a glance at me.

"Yes, I'm all right," I said.

"Good, then watch out for that bloody house… "

I pulled up on the stick and we roared over the roof of a local farmhouse.

"Not far now," Maria said, giving out a new bearing.

The flight turned as one and then we were on a direct line for the target. More fields flashed by as the sky became steadily lighter. We aimed to hit the target before sunrise. It looked like we were going to make it.

The pre-dawn light made it easier for us to see our way as the quiet world unfolded below us. Hopefully, the Germans would not be alert at that time of day. They certainly wouldn't be expecting us.

"Split in five," Maria said suddenly.

The moment was here. We were almost ready to start the attack run. My heart rate shot up.

"Split in one," said Maria.

That was it. I gave the order to split into two teams. We'd fly in from different sides of the airfield. Alpha would go first, and then Beta.

"Wildcats, split. Alphas on me," I said, banking to the right.

"Betas on me," said Linda, taking the other half the squadron away to the left.

"Big Show eight o'clock," said Maria.

Sure enough, there it was: the airfield, the runway and the buildings, with two neat rows of fighters parked on the grass. Fortunately, there was no sign of life.

"Let's get this done," I said, feeling a surge of adrenaline.

I took the team wide of the airfield and then turned back towards it.

"Alphas attack formation," I said as the rest of the team fanned out in a line.

We were approaching the runway at an angle, ready to drop the ordnance then turn clear and come back for another attack run. As soon as we'd dropped our bombs, Beta would fly in from the opposite side. The fuses were on a long timer to give both teams time to drop the bombs before they detonated.

"Runway coming up," said Maria.

My heart was racing. I slipped off the safety on the guns, my finger poised over the bomb release. All of our training, all of the hours had come down to this one defining moment.

My mind was focused as we roared across the fields at low level. When we were almost over the runway, Maria called it.

"Now," she said.

I released the deadly payload. "Alphas, bombs away," I said.

We turned rapidly away from the airfield. Beta team took their cue from us.

"Betas, attack formation," I heard Linda say.

We waited to hear that Linda's team had released their ordnance too. Seconds flew by and then finally I heard her say, "Betas, bombs away."

"Alphas on me, strafing run," I said, turning back to the airfield. The Beta team was heading towards us; they would attack behind us when we'd cleared the field a second time. The Betas were just out of the airfield when all hell broke loose.

The bombs from twelve aircraft went off almost simultaneously, throwing up a massive fireball. Smoke began pouring from the buildings. I could see figures running.

"Alphas, attack formation," I said. We spread out to strafe the airfield. The line of Focke-Wulfs was in our sights.

Without warning, a machine gun opened up from the airfield perimeter. Streams of tracers shot past the canopy.

"Christ!" said Maria.

"Alphas, stay on target," I said. "Take out the planes."

We had never been under fire before, but somehow I kept my cool as a stream of bullets came our way. I waited with my finger poised on the fire button until we were close enough.

I could see the machine gun post at the edge of the field. If we were lucky, we might get that too. I gave the order.

"Alphas … fire!"

The cannons from six Mosquitos tore up the dirt. The machine gun ceased its chatter as the bullets took it down. The next moment, the Wulfs were exploding like fireworks, hit by the high-calibre cannon fire. We passed over the burning airfield and I took us away to the left to give Beta team a clear strafing run. There was no feeling of satisfaction, no time to think about it, just the sheer will to finish the job and be gone.

"Betas, fire," I heard Linda say as the Beta team swooped in across the field.

"Damn it, there's another gun," said Patricia.

Sure enough, another emplacement was firing at the fleeing Beta team. I hoped they would get away before any of them was hit. Just then, a voice came over the radio.

"Wildcat Leader, I'm going to take out the gun." It was Carol.

Before I could say anything, her plane left formation and flew back towards the airfield. She opened fire on the gun, which turned its attention to her. This wasn't in the plan. The plan was to carry out the attack and then get away as fast as possible.

"Wildcat Ten, disengage, I repeat, disengage," I said. "Wildcats to the rendezvous." I turned the flight formation from the scene, hoping Carol would heed my orders.

"What the hell is she thinking?" said Maria.

"I don't know, but I've got eleven other planes to get home," I told her. I didn't like the thought of leaving someone behind.

As we rapidly flew away from the scene, Carol called in. It was the one thing I hadn't wanted to hear.

"We're hit, we're hit," she said.

"Wildcat Ten, can you get to the rendezvous?"

"Yes, I can see you up ahead, but my navigator's been hit… She's bleeding… What should I do?"

Maria and I looked at each other. The navigator was ASO Frances York. There was nothing we could do about it.

"Step on it and get in formation, Wildcat Ten," I said.

We had made the rendezvous point with Beta and there was no choice but to get going.

I felt a hand on my arm.

"Anna, we've got to get home," said Maria, gently. "We're counting on you to get us home."

I nodded; we had no choice. I hoped Carol would catch us.

"Wildcats, form up on me. Let's go home."

"Wildcat Ten on station…" It was Carol.

I breathed a sigh of relief. Maria gave the bearing and I opened up the throttle. We had lost precious minutes. The ground batteries would be on high alert now that we'd carried out the raid.

"Wildcats, let's get the hell out of here," I said over the radio.

The return journey was nothing like the inbound light. On the way in the enemy hadn't been expecting us. Now they knew all about it. We'd left quite a calling card on their doorstep. The Jerries might scramble their fighters and come in pursuit. If they caught us, we were all done for.

"Lines, for Christ's sake, lines!" Maria cut in.

"I've seen them. Calm down," I retorted.

"I'm trying," she said.

"Then keep a lookout for Jerry."

"I'm looking out for *you*," she said.

We were wound up, fraught and tired, and it was taking its toll. Then I had an idea. "Sing for me," I said to Maria.

"What?"

"Sing, to keep me awake."

Maria started up a passable rendition of 'Men of Harlech', which I found quite stirring. It helped me to settle and focus.

The miles flew by, hedge after hedge, tree after tree, and all the while the sky grew lighter until suddenly the sun burst out in all its glory. The landscape took on a golden hue.

"How long do I have to keep singing for?" Maria demanded, having been through all the verses twice.

"You can stop now," I said, laughing.

Connie's voice burst over the radio, shattering the calm. "Bandits, six o'clock."

"That's all we bloody need," said Maria.

"How far, Wildcat Two?" I asked Connie.

"Not far enough."

"Wildcats, lets push the speed all the way up — we can outrun them," I told the others.

"Wilco," came the responses.

I watched the airspeed climbing and the kite felt like it was really starting to move with the land flying past below us.

We left the French coast in short order. I kept us fast and low. There was shipping to the left and right, but not so close that we had to avoid them.

"Those are our destroyers," said Maria.

"Perhaps they'll scare off the Jerries," I said. "Wildcat Two, how are those bandits?"

"Still coming," said Connie. "But I think we're losing them… Oh! The ships have opened fire."

"Phew," said Maria.

"They bandits are turning back to France," said Connie.

I breathed a sigh of relief as the British coastline loomed up in front of us. Once we made landfall, I took us a little higher, so we didn't have to work quite so hard. I finally had time to think about Carol and Frances.

"Wildcat Ten," I said. "How's your navigator?"

"She didn't make it," came the reply.

"Roger, I'm sorry."

I felt suddenly numb. One of us had died. I told myself that this was the reality of war and forced my mind back on the job. We were still on high alert.

"Control, this is Wildcat Leader. We're coming in. Requesting permission to land."

"Roger, Wildcat Leader, you're clear," said Control.

"One casualty on board," I told them.

"Do they need a medic?"

"Negative," I replied.

"Roger."

The familiar sight of Hawberry Hall and the airfield came into view. We lined up for the final approach one by one, with our plane going first. The next moment, the wheels touched the ground. Finally, we were safe.

"Woohoo! We did it," said Maria as we landed. "I can't believe we did it."

"Yes," I replied, suddenly exhausted. "Yes, we did."

I taxied to the standings and then a wave of emotion hit me. For a few moments, I sat there with tears streaming down my face.

"It's all right, Anna. We're home," said Maria softly. She handed me a handkerchief.

"I know, it's just… What if we hadn't … we could have —"

She gently cut me short. "What happened to Frances wasn't your fault. You've done your duty, and that's all that matters."

I nodded and managed a small smile.

"Now, if you're ready to face the world, let's go. And you can keep that," Maria said, indicating the handkerchief.

The ground crew were waiting with James, Henry and Gloria. As we jumped down from the plane to join the other Sirens, they started to applaud us.

"Anna, we did it! We made it," said Jennifer, running up to hug me tightly.

I returned the embrace and suddenly we were all hugging, patting each other on the back and laughing. Our welcoming committee waited patiently, and then James stepped forward. He was grinning from ear to ear.

"Well done, Anna. You did a magnificent job," he said, shaking my hand.

"Thank you, sir," I said, returning the smile.

He moved on, thanking each member of the team in turn, as did the others. There was excited chatter for a few moments. I let it all swirl around me, feeling a little overwhelmed.

"Let's get back to Hawberry," said Gloria loudly, cutting into the celebrations. "We've got food laid on."

"Great," said Connie. "I'm famished."

We piled into the waiting trucks. Connie sat at the back with Jennifer, as usual. She lit a cigarette and took a long, satisfied pull on it.

"Finally! I've been gasping for a smoke," she said, handing it to Jennifer.

"It was quite something, don't you think, the mission?" said Patricia.

"Did you see the way those planes exploded?" Shelly put in. "It was better than bonfire night."

In the dining room, a spread had been laid on. Roast beef with all the trimmings, followed by sponge pudding and custard. James told us he'd asked the kitchens to keep it aside for an occasion like this. He promised us a debrief the next morning and after dinner, I went up to my room. Some of the others went to the house bar for a drink. They tried to persuade me to join them, but I wasn't in the mood. Instead, I had a bath and went to bed.

I was almost asleep when Jennifer entered the room.

"Are you still awake?" she whispered, changing into her night clothes.

"Yes."

"You did well today, Anna," she told me, sliding under the covers and holding me tight.

"Did I?"

"Yes, you did. And what happened to Frances was not your fault. Carol didn't follow orders. Everyone heard her."

"I know," I said. "But I still can't help feeling responsible."

"Well, don't. You did everything right." She began to sing softly. It was the lullaby our mother used to sing to us when we were young. My thoughts drifted back to earlier times before the war, when we didn't have a care in the world. I finally closed my eyes and went to sleep.

CHAPTER THIRTEEN

The following morning at breakfast, the talk was all about the mission.

"I don't care what Linda says, Anna, you did a fantastic job," said Connie, cutting into her eggs.

"For goodness' sake," hissed Patricia. "Why did you have to go and open your mouth?"

I looked up from my plate. Up until that point, I had been enjoying my breakfast.

"Go on, you might as well tell me. What did Linda say?" I asked.

"It doesn't matter," said Connie.

"Yes, it does," I said. "You brought it up and I have a right to know."

I waited for someone to speak. Instead, the others exchanged anxious glances.

I laid down my fork. "Well?" I demanded.

"You're right, you should know," said Maria at last. "Linda's saying that you bungled the mission."

"What?" I stared at her.

"She said you didn't have proper control over your team, and that's why Carol attacked the machine gun. You waited too long before leaving, we could all have been killed, and if *she'd* been in charge, Frances wouldn't have died."

I took a deep breath. "Anything else?" I asked.

"No, that's about it," said Maria, eyeing me with some misgiving.

I stood up, pushing my chair back loudly. "I've had enough of this," I told them. "I'm going to have it out with Linda."

"Anna, think before you —" Jennifer began, but I was in no mood to listen.

I spied Linda at a table in the corner and strode towards her, determined to give her a piece of my mind. I was halfway across the dining room when Judy intercepted me.

"The Wing Commander wants to see you, ma'am," she said.

"What?" I said, stopping in my tracks. "Now?"

"Yes, ma'am. Right now," she continued. "He was most insistent."

This rather took the wind out of my sails. There was nothing for it but to obey the summons from the CO.

"Oh … right, well, I suppose I'll come then."

"Follow me," she said, rapidly leading the way out of the dining room.

As we walked along the corridors, I was still feeling extremely miffed, but my initial anger began to dissipate. What if what Linda had said was true? What if Frances's death really was all my fault? What if I wasn't fit to lead the flight?

We reached James's office, and Judy ushered me in and closed the door behind us. Seated at the meeting table were James, Henry and Gloria. It was time to face the music.

"Anna, please have a seat," said James pleasantly, indicating a chair on the opposite side of the table.

I saluted and sat down with my hands clutched in my lap.

"No need to look so serious," said James. "We're not going to bite."

I smiled faintly, but the situation was making me nervous, particularly after what I had just heard at the breakfast table. Was this going to be an inquisition?

"We would like you to tell us how the mission went from your perspective. I'm sure you will have some valuable insights," James said. "So, how did it go?"

"From the beginning?" I asked.

"That would be a good place to start."

He smiled disarmingly and so I furnished them with an account of the raid from the moment of take-off. They listened without comment.

"Firstly," James said, when I'd finished, "I want to say, very well done."

I was immediately flustered by this praise. "Oh … well … I…"

"You did a superb job," he continued. "You carried out the mission just as well as we'd hoped — better, in fact."

"So, you don't think that Frances's death was my fault?" I blurted out before I could stop myself.

"What? No. Who said that?" said James sharply.

"I … I wouldn't like to say," I said lamely, not wanting to drop Linda in it, even though she seemed to have declared herself my rival.

"I think I can guess," Gloria told him. She had probably heard the gossip already.

"Right," said James. "I see. Well, to answer your question, in no way was ASO York's death your fault. Nor is it your fault that SO Henderson didn't follow orders."

"These things happen on missions," said Henry sympathetically. "We're all human and sometimes people act unwisely, thinking they're helping the situation when they're not."

"Right," I said, relieved to hear that was what they thought. "Thank you."

"In any case," said James, "we've come to a decision. In fact, it's one that I'd made a while back, but for the sake of protocol we wanted to wait until you'd led your first mission."

"A decision?" I felt a little nonplussed.

"Yes, I think — we all think — that you can't lead the flight without a proper rank, so we're promoting you to Flight Officer."

I stared at him. "What? I mean … thank you," I said, a little flustered. The promotion was entirely unexpected.

"It's effective immediately and, accordingly — Gloria, would you do the honours?"

Gloria stood up and went over to a small table, where I noticed there was a folded Air Force jacket. She picked it up and walked over to me.

"Here," she said, smiling. "You can take off your jacket and put this on. It's in your size."

The jacket had the Flight Officer insignia on it. I put it on and buttoned it up.

"Very smart too," said James approvingly. "And congratulations, Flight Officer Nightingale."

"Well deserved," said Gloria, returning to her seat.

"Will that be all, sir?" I asked James, blushing under his gaze.

"Yes, Anna, that's all for now. We'll hold a briefing shortly."

"We've got your back, Anna," said Gloria.

"Thank you," I said, snapping them a smart salute.

As I left the room, Judy whispered, "Well done, ma'am, I'm thrilled for you."

I wasn't used to being the centre of attention. However, now I was a Flight Officer and confirmed as Flight Leader, the spotlight would always be firmly on me. Just like the jacket, I was going to have to wear it.

I rounded a corner of the corridor and walked slap-bang into the others.

"We came to find out what happened —" Shelly began. Her eyes widened. "You've been promoted!" she cried, beaming from ear to ear.

"Yes, I'm Flight Officer Nightingale now," I said, smiling too.

"Wow! A Flight Officer!" said Jennifer proudly, giving me a hug.

"It was quite a surprise, I have to say," I told them.

"Not to us," said Patricia. "You're the leader, and now you've got the rank to prove it."

I was about to respond when I heard a voice behind me.

"I hear you're looking for me, Anna Nightingale. Well, here I am."

It was Linda. The others looked at me.

"I'll deal with this," I said quietly.

They say that revenge is a dish best served cold, and I was more than ready to serve it. I turned around to face her. Linda was standing a short distance away with ASO Janice Kipling, SO Ruth Maddison and ASO Brenda Biggins.

She looked me up and down in a contemptuous way and then her eyes suddenly widened when she saw my rank. I didn't give her the chance to speak. I hadn't been drilled by Sergeant Wallace for nothing.

"Stand to attention when you're addressing a senior officer!" I barked out in a parade ground voice I didn't know I possessed. "Have you forgotten how to salute, Section Officer?"

Linda snapped to attention, as did the others beside her.

I saluted her back smartly. "Now, what is it you wanted to say to me? Something about the mission, was it?" I asked.

There was an infinitesimal moment where she looked as if she would give me an unwise retort, and then she must have quelled the impulse.

"Nothing, ma'am," she replied. "Nothing at all."

"Good," I said. "See that it stays that way."

"Yes, ma'am," she said.

"Dismissed."

She saluted again and walked rapidly away with her friends. A cheer erupted behind me.

"Bloody good job," said Maria.

"You showed her!" said Connie with satisfaction.

"Did you see her face when she saw your rank?" said Patricia, laughing.

I couldn't help laughing along with the others.

Jennifer slipped her arm through mine. "I'm proud of you, Anna, for standing up for yourself like that."

"We're going out tonight to celebrate," Maria informed me. "And you're not going to say no."

"All right, fine," I said. "In the meantime, James said there was going to be a briefing. Come on or we'll all be late."

Our spirits high, we made our way to the briefing room.

There was a buzz of conversation, which ceased when we arrived. Some glanced in my direction, then quickly looked away.

We took seats near the front. Now I had the rank, I had to live up to it. Shortly afterwards, James entered with Gloria and Henry. We stood to attention while they took the podium.

"At ease," said James.

He waited until we were seated once more and then began. "First of all, I would like to congratulate you all on a job well done. You have exceeded our expectations for the mission. You have ably demonstrated that the Sirens are a deadly force to be reckoned with. We are proud of you, and your exploits will not have gone unnoticed in the right quarters."

Henry stepped forward. "Intelligence reports indicate a high level of success. All the German planes were destroyed, many of the airport buildings, and the runway damaged. It will take some time for the airbase to become operational once more."

"Thank you, Henry," said James. "We'd also like to express a particular thank you to our Flight Leader, Anna Nightingale." He paused, looking directly at me. "For those of you who don't know, she has been promoted to Flight Officer. She did an excellent job on this mission, and the flight could not be in better hands. We look forward to her continuing to lead further successful missions."

Maria shot me a triumphant look and Jennifer squeezed my hand.

"We have some more excellent news," James continued. "This mission was something of a watershed … to convince, let's say, the unbelievers. Now that you have proven yourselves to be everything we said you would be, the Sirens have become officially endorsed. You will remain one of the best kept secrets of the war, but it does mean that we'll very likely be increasing your numbers in due course."

I wondered what that meant. Another squadron? I didn't have time to muse on it, because James was still talking.

"It also means that we can finally issue our unofficial insignia. A badge, if you like, of honour. These will be distributed as a patch that you can sew onto your uniforms and flying jackets, and also as metal pins you can wear on your lapel. A reminder of who you are and what we stand for."

This pronouncement brought quite a few smiles. It gave us an identity. I wondered what the insignia might be.

"If you go and see Sergeant Wallace after the briefing, you can collect your badges and pins," James said. "Finally, I must come to the sad loss of ASO Frances York, who was killed in action on the mission. An official funeral for Frances will be held this week. She will be buried in the grounds of Hawberry

Hall near the chapel. Her family has been informed that she died in a tragic flying accident while transporting a plane."

The room had fallen silent at this stark reminder of the consequences of war.

"Nobody is to blame for her loss," James continued. "In the heat of the moment, things happen. This was, after all, the first time any of you have been under fire. Try, if you can, to stick to the mission orders. We will lay Frances to rest in the manner fitting a member of this squadron and be glad that the rest of you live to fight another day."

I looked over at Carol. She was staring at the floor. She probably blamed herself for what had happened. I wondered if I should try to talk to her.

"You're probably wondering what happens next," James said. "Firstly, we are recruiting another navigator, and we will continue training because that's what keeps us all sharp. There is another mission being planned very soon. Specialised training will be required for that. In other words, carry on … that's what we will all do until this war is won. Today, however, collect your badges and take the rest of the day off. You've earned it. Thank you."

James left the stage along with the others. When they had gone, we all went over to the table where Sergeant Wallace was standing.

"Now ladies," she told us, "form an orderly queue — senior officers first."

I duly went to the head of the queue and picked up my badges and pin. I was quickly followed by the others, then we all stood around examining them excitedly.

The insignia consisted of a mermaid with the word 'Sirens' printed in capitals above. It was a simple design and I thought it rather splendid.

"Well, I like it," said Maria, once we were together in our little group.

"Very classy," said Connie, putting the pin on her lapel.

The rest of us followed suit and then discussed going back to my room for a sewing party.

"So have I got to call you ma'am, now?" asked Jennifer with a grin as we all walked upstairs.

"Only when you have to," I replied, smiling back at her.

"Right you are, ma'am," said Connie.

"Stop it, all of you," I said. "I'm still me and we're still friends."

"We're more than just friends," said Shelly. "We're the Sirens."

It was true. We were a sisterhood and a deadly one at that.

That evening we repaired to the local pub, the Dog and Trumpet. We had spent the afternoon sewing the badges onto our uniforms, laughing, joking and having a good time. I didn't really want to go out, but I couldn't refuse because the others wanted to toast my promotion.

We sat around a table in the saloon bar supping pints, while Connie and Jennifer smoked. It was a typical country pub, with two bars and a lively atmosphere.

Over in another part of the bar sat a small group of RAF pilots who were being rather rowdy. One or two of them kept flicking glances in our direction.

"Wait for it," said Shelly. "One of them is going to come over here at any moment."

"How do you know that?" I asked her.

"In the ways of men, Shelly is an expert," said Maria sardonically.

The others laughed.

"Here we go, what did I say?" said Shelly in a low voice.

Sure enough, one of the pilots, a Flying Officer, had got up from their table and wandered over.

"Hello, ladies," he said affably. "My friends over there were wondering if you'd join us for a drink."

"I don't know," said Shelly. "Are you offering to *buy* us a drink?"

"Sure, what would you ladies like? Flying Officer Neville Smith, by the way," he said, introducing himself with a disarming smile.

"You can get us a round, then your lot can come and join *us*," Shelly told him.

We watched him return to his table and talk to the other pilots, who let out a cheer.

They joined us at our table while Neville went up to the bar to order the drinks. He had blond hair and sported a natty moustache. We soon discovered that they were from a nearby Hurricane squadron.

As drinks were consumed, they began to tell us about their exploits.

"So there was this 109 coming at me, I rolled right under him and then I got him in my sights…"

"You should have seen it, five Focke-Wulfs, five… It was pretty much touch and go…"

"I had him in my sights and fired. He went down in flames … boom … just like that — you should have seen it…"

We sat listening patiently while Shelly made suitably appreciative noises. She turned and winked at us as one of the pilots told us a particularly involved story about how he had shot down a Heinkel.

After a while, the conversation petered out. A Pilot Officer named Harold Carpenter asked, "So what do you ladies do? You're in the WAAF, right?"

"Yes," said Jennifer, "that's right. We transport planes."

"What's that badge on your arm?" asked another pilot, whose name was Charlie King. "The Sirens?"

"That's our nickname," said Maria casually.

"I'm going outside to get some air," I announced suddenly. The smoky atmosphere was starting to give me a headache.

"Are you all right?" asked Maria at once.

"I'm fine. I'll just be a few minutes."

I left them to it and went to stand outside at the front of the pub. The night air was crisp. I took a deep breath, thankful for the freshness. It had been quite a day, and listening to those pilots had been dispiriting. Instead of joining in with the tales of derring-do, we'd had to lie about ourselves.

Perhaps this was our lot. We'd never get to tell anyone of our exploits and people would assume that we transported planes. It was all to the good for preserving our cover, but it still felt unfair.

I was just thinking about going back inside when there was a voice beside me. I had been lost in my thoughts. I looked around and saw it was Charlie.

"Hello," he said. "What are you doing out here all alone?" His speech was a little slurred.

"I'm just getting some air," I replied.

"Aren't you cold?" he asked, moving closer.

"No, I'm fine."

"Here, let me help you warm up."

Without warning, he put his arm around me. I shrugged it off at once. "Don't," I said.

"Oh, come on," he said, trying again.

I pushed him away from me. "I said don't."

I heard a car driving by. It drew up and someone got out.

"I suggest you leave the Flight Officer alone," said a familiar voice. It was James.

"Who are you?" Charlie asked, frowning.

"Wing Commander James Donnington," said James in an icy tone. "Stand to attention when I'm talking to you."

Charlie stood to attention with difficulty and gave a sloppy salute.

"You're drunk," said James. "Now, I suggest you apologise to my officer — a *senior* officer, by the way — and get back inside. Otherwise, I'm happy to call the Military Police. Whichever you prefer."

"That won't be necessary, sir," said Charlie, turning to me. "Ma'am, I am sorry for my behaviour. It was out of order."

"That's all right," I replied, then, "See it doesn't happen again."

"If it does, I'll be speaking to your commanding officer," added James.

"Yes, sir, it won't happen again," said Charlie, looking abashed.

"Right then, dismissed."

Charlie left the scene briskly and James stepped forward.

"Anna," he said, his tone altogether softer. "Are you hurt?"

"No," I said. "Thank you for stopping."

"I happened to be driving past when I saw what was happening."

I was grateful. I hadn't been sure what to do; I wasn't used to unwanted male attention.

"Let me give you a lift back to base," James offered. "If you're ready to go, that is?"

I hesitated. "Would you mind waiting while I tell the others? They'll be worried otherwise."

"Of course," said James. "I'll wait in the car."

I went back inside the pub. There were some enquiring looks from Maria and Jennifer. Charlie was sitting at the table. He avoided my eyes.

"I'm going back," I told the others. "James has offered me a lift."

"James?" said Maria in surprise.

"Yes, he was passing by and…" I trailed off.

"Is something the matter, Anna?" asked Jennifer.

"I'll tell you later," I said.

"I think we'll go too," said Shelly. "It's about that time anyway."

"Will we see you again?" asked Harold.

"I don't know, will you?" Maria replied with a smile.

"Shame you ladies won't get to find out what it's like to fly against Jerry," said Charlie, his voice mocking.

Shelly came back at him, quick as a flash. "Well, you know what they say," she said sweetly, "the female of the species is deadlier than the male."

"That might be true, but you'll never get a chance to prove it in combat," he said, belligerently.

"No, you're right. But if we did, I assure you, darling, we'd be twice as lethal as you lot."

With that, we turned and left. Outside the pub, we collapsed with laughter.

"Did you see their faces?"

"If only they knew…"

"Go on, Anna," said Maria, giving me a gentle nudge. "James is waiting."

CHAPTER FOURTEEN

In the car, James was solicitous. We talked a little bit about the mission and the pilots in the pub. He laughed when I told him how the pilots had been bragging.

"Boys will be boys," he said. "Always trying to impress the ladies."

I was silent for a few moments before James broke in on my thoughts.

"Penny for them?" he said.

"Sorry, it's been a long day, sir," I said, prevaricating. "That's all."

"I understand," he said.

It felt as if there was more he wanted to say, but instead we talked about the war.

When we arrived at Hawberry, we walked inside together. James bade me goodnight and I watched him walk away with something of a pang. I found him both charming and genuine.

Back in my room, the others were waiting.

"Well?" said Maria. "What happened? We need to know."

I told them about Charlie and Connie fired up immediately.

"How dare he!" she said. "I'd like to give him a piece of my mind."

"It's all right, really it is," I said.

"Only because James came along when he did," Patricia pointed out.

"Next time, you give him a thump right where it hurts," Shelly said with a decisive nod. We all laughed at this.

"So, what happened with James?" Maria asked me.

"Nothing happened with James," I replied. "He's the CO. I mean, how would it look? What would the others say?"

"Who cares what they say?" said Patricia.

Jennifer and Connie were sitting by the window smoking. The window was slightly ajar to let the smoke out. Jennifer took a drag and handed the cigarette to Connie.

"Are you falling in love with him, though, even just a little?" Jennifer asked me bluntly.

"I…" I felt a flush rising to my face.

Maria saw my discomfort and came to my rescue. "Leave her alone, you lot. She has to make her own decisions," she told them. "Isn't that right, Anna?"

I shot her a grateful smile. The party broke up soon after and I went to bed. Jennifer joined me, but no more was said about James.

The following morning another briefing was called. We assembled once more in the briefing room. I sat at the front again with my colleagues. To be a leader, I needed to be seen to be a leader.

The briefing started shortly after James, Henry, Gloria and the Marx Brothers took to the podium.

"Welcome," said James, "to the next phase of our deployment."

This got everyone's attention.

"We will soon have a new mission. What we're about to tell you is top secret and must not leave this room," he continued. "The mission will require some new skills on the part of some of you. I will now hand over to our MI6 colleagues to elaborate."

He sat down while Harpo and Chico stood up. Harpo motioned to the projectionist at the back of the room and the lights were dimmed. The screen had been pulled down to allow slides to be projected onto it.

"You know, of course, about the Gestapo," he said.

There were murmurs of assent; we had been well briefed on their horrific methods.

"What you may not have heard of, because few have, is the *Carlingue*, or French Gestapo."

He motioned to the projectionist and a slide appeared on the screen, showing three men.

"The *Carlingue* are French auxiliaries operating under the Gestapo banner. It was created by these three men, Pierre Bonny, Henri Lafont and Pierre Loutrel, all notorious criminals in the French underworld. Bonny was a former policeman who, to put it politely, went rogue."

Harpo took a drag from his cigarette and Chico continued.

"They use the same methods of torture as the Gestapo. To all intents and purposes they can be regarded as the same organisation, apart from the fact that these men and all who work for them are traitors to France and to their countrymen."

A new slide appeared, showing the frontage of a building.

"Number 93, Rue Lauriston in Paris, their headquarters," Harpo said, indicating the photograph. "But *that* is not our target."

"No," said Chico. "Our target has yet to be confirmed, but we believe it will be a secret location in Rouen. Certain prisoners of the *Carlingue* and the Gestapo are due to be moved to this secret location for special interrogation. Currently, we understand that the facilities are still being built."

A slide came up showing some buildings under construction. Harpo's expression was grim.

"We won't bore you with the details of the interrogation methods, but we can assure you that they are not pleasant. We also believe it's highly likely that as a result, those being questioned will reveal the vital information they are holding."

"We can't allow this information to be revealed at any cost," said Chico. "Some of those being held know the names of other operatives in the Resistance, locations of safehouses, plans for future operations and more. As such, we have no choice but to neutralise this threat."

This could mean only one thing and Harpo spelt it out.

"Once the transfer of prisoners takes place, your mission will be to wipe out the facility and everyone in it."

You could have heard a pin drop at this announcement. The two spies paused to stub out their cigarettes and light up two more. Harpo took a long drag on his while Chico spoke.

"Let me be clear," he said. "In addition to the war criminals — the *Carlingue* and the Gestapo — this target will house operatives who are brothers, sisters, cousins, husbands and wives to our own people, British spies working undercover in enemy territory, as well as French men and women from the Resistance. All of them were captured by the Germans and are awaiting interrogation designed to make them crack. And crack they will. So, we cannot hesitate to act. You, the Sirens, cannot hesitate to act when the time comes."

"A few must die to save the many," said Harpo. "We are depending on you all to do your duty to King and Country and save these people from an otherwise much worse fate."

It was a stark dilemma. We had to kill our own to save our own. I was filled with misgivings about what we were being called on to do.

Harpo and Chico sat down. James stood up. The lights came back on.

"Sometimes," he said, "we have to make hard choices. You all made a choice to be part of the Sirens. That choice comes with the obligation to do your duty no matter what. I am certain that you will all do your duty now, just as you did in the last mission."

I glanced at the pale faces around me. If any of us had harboured a romanticised view of the war, we were thoroughly disabused of it now.

"To practical matters," said Henry, stepping forward. "The target will be well defended, and that's why this squadron has been chosen for the mission. We could send in several waves of bombers to try and flatten the site, but they will be doing so through heavy flak and no doubt German fighters. A stealth mission with a precision strike has a far higher chance of success. By the time the mission comes around, we will know exactly where to attack the prison complex.

"As you have already heard, the facility is still under construction. So, the prisoners will not be moved there until it is ready. They are being held at various locations around France and we can't strike until they are all at the target. The mission itself will be carried out at night. Two of our Mosquitos will be fitted with new onboard radar to allow you to detect enemy fighters. However, the aim of the mission is to get in and out again as fast as possible."

"There will be no second chances," Henry continued. "If we get this wrong, the Germans will know we've found out about the facility and they will dissipate their prisoners all over France once more. Our opportunity will have been lost."

"Now for the good news," said James with a smile.

This was greeted by laughter, which helped to release the tension we were all feeling.

"A new navigator will join us shortly and attend your training. We are also currently recruiting pilots and navigators to form a reserve pool for this squadron. They will be undergoing the same training you did, and I'm sure when they arrive you will make them feel welcome." He looked around. "Any questions?" When there were none, he continued, "All right then. The funeral service for Frances will be held in two days. Funeral duties will be posted up and Sergeant Wallace will conduct rehearsals for the guard of honour."

CHAPTER FIFTEEN

We were back into the familiar routine of training: refreshing our flying skills, basic navigation and flying exercises. The next day we headed out in the trucks to the airfield.

"Why do we have to keep doing the same thing?" complained Connie, tapping the ash from her cigarette over the back of the truck.

"Because we have to stay sharp," I told her. "You heard what James said: we have to be mission fit."

"Besides which, they're not going to have us sitting around all day on our backsides," observed Maria.

"Would you rather do drill, Connie?" asked Shelly.

"No, I bloody well would not," said Connie emphatically.

We all laughed.

The truck came to a stop. We jumped out and walked over to the planes, where Henry was waiting for us. A new woman was with him.

"I'd like to introduce ASO Rose Mallory," said Henry. "She'll be navigating for Carol."

"Follow our lead, listen out for the bearings and you'll be all right," Maria told her.

"Thank you," said Rose, looking a little nervous.

"You'll do fine," said Maria with a reassuring smile.

"This is a routine low-flying run," Henry said. "Stick to the course and waypoints, then come back. All right?"

"Yes, sir," we all responded.

"All right, Sirens," I said. "Let's get to it."

I climbed up into the cockpit of our Mosquito, followed by Maria.

"Back in the saddle," she said, strapping herself in.

It seemed strange. The mission felt like a dream now it was over. "Let's wind her up," I said, starting the Mosquito engines.

Once they were purring nicely, I checked in with the rest of the flight.

"Bluebird Two ready."

"Bluebird Three ready."

When we got to Bluebird Eleven, I taxied the kite down towards the end of the runway.

"Control, this is Bluebird Leader requesting permission to take off," I said.

"Bluebird Leader, you're clear," came the response.

I opened up the throttle and we set off down the runway, gathering speed. In a few moments we were airborne and circling, waiting for the others to join us. Once the squadron was in the air, we were ready.

"Bluebirds, close formation, low-level flying, let's go."

Maria gave out the bearing and I dropped down to hedge-hopping height. It was all too familiar as the ground began flashing below us once more.

"Here we go," said Maria. "And there's a house."

"Seen it."

She laughed. The low flying seemed somehow easier now and more relaxed in practice. I took in the terrain a lot quicker and reacted a lot faster. Perhaps it was all a matter of repetition. Perhaps it was the fact that we'd finally flown a mission.

"Treeline," said Maria.

"Got it."

The group seemed to be flying as one. I was just thinking about congratulating everyone on their precision when we got back to base, when Jennifer hit a problem.

"Bluebird Leader, my engines are losing power. I don't know what's wrong," she said.

"Return to base, Bluebird Four," I told her.

"Wilco," she said, dropping out of formation.

We carried on to the next waypoint. Up and down over trees, hedges, telegraph lines. Moments later, Patricia hit a snag.

"Bluebird Leader," she said. "We've got a stutter on the starboard engine — it keeps cutting out. We can't keep up."

I looked at Maria and her face mirrored my concern. One problem was unlucky, but two seemed too much of a coincidence. The Mosquitos were regularly maintained and kept airworthy. Up until now, we'd never had a mechanical problem. I made a decision to stop the practice.

"Abort, Bluebirds, abort, we're returning to base. Bluebird Two, get back to base as soon as you can."

I wheeled the flight around and Maria gave us a bearing for home.

"Bluebird Leader, we're nearly there," said Jennifer over the radio as we flew towards Hawberry.

She had made it back, but the next moment she radioed in again.

"The engines have cut out. I'm gliding it in; wish me luck." I could hear a slight note of panic in her voice. If she was worried, then that was not a good sign.

"Easy, Jenny, easy," I said, forgetting to use the call sign in my concern.

"We're coming down a little fast but … oh, blast … damn it … yes … got it … thank God for that… We're down. We made it."

I released the breath I hadn't realised I'd been holding whilst listening to Jennifer over the radio.

"Focus, Anna, focus," said Maria. "Jennifer's all right; now you need to get us all back to base … and remember to breathe."

I could always rely on Maria to keep me grounded and I was grateful for it.

"Bluebird Two, how are you doing?" I asked Patricia.

"The engine is just about holding up, Bluebird Leader. Sounds like something in the fuel line, maybe a blockage."

"Roger, Bluebird Two. Let me know if anything changes."

"Wilco."

The airfield came into view, and I radioed in. "Control, this is Bluebird Leader requesting permission to land," I said.

"You're clear, Bluebird Leader. Do you need a tender on standby for Bluebird Two?" Control asked.

"Might be wise, although they're not in difficulty at the moment."

"Roger," said Control.

I took us down in short order, followed by the rest of the flight. As soon as we'd jumped down from the plane, I walked over to where Jennifer and Shelly were talking to one of the mechanics.

"Ma'am," said Leading Aircraftwoman Victoria Singleton with a salute. She was wearing overalls and had a grease smudge on her face. "I suppose you want to know what's wrong with SO Nightingale's plane?"

I didn't know the mechanics particularly well. With so many personnel on the base, it was hard to keep up with names, let alone get to know them all.

"Yes," I said. "We've also got another one coming in with an engine stutter."

"I don't understand it," said Victoria. "We go over the kites every day. Anything dodgy is replaced, particularly before a mission."

"I see," I replied. "So it's a bit strange that we have two planes with problems?"

"Yes, ma'am, it certainly is. I'm not sure what to make of it. But not to worry, we'll go over them with a fine-tooth comb and let you know."

"All right," I said. "We have another practice flight tomorrow. We need them airworthy by then."

"Of course, ma'am," said Victoria.

"Coming?" I asked Jennifer.

"I'll stay for a bit," she said.

"I'll stay too," said Connie, who had sauntered up to us unnoticed.

"As you wish."

I exchanged salutes with Victoria and left them to it. As Maria and I headed for the trucks, we were joined by Shelly.

"Aren't you staying?" Maria asked.

"Two's company, three's a crowd," said Shelly.

"Oh, right," said Maria, flicking a glance back to where Jennifer and Connie were still chatting to Victoria.

We returned to base in the trucks. Patricia joined us, having got her plane down safely.

"It seems incredibly unlucky to have two planes go wrong at the same time," said Susan.

"Yes," I agreed. "But we don't know if it was anything more than that."

"What more could it be?" Shelly asked me.

I shrugged.

"Things wear out, don't they?" said Maria.

"Yes," I said. "Yes, they do, but these planes are not that old."

"We've been flying them a lot, though," she replied.

There wasn't any point in dwelling on it. I'd find out from Victoria the next day what was amiss.

The following morning, we were due to run more low-flying drills. When we arrived at the airfield, I made a point of going to speak to Victoria. I went with Maria to seek her out in one of the hangars.

"Ma'am," Victoria said, returning my salute. "The two aircraft are back in action for you."

"That's great," I replied. "What was the problem?"

She sighed. "I'm not entirely sure. The stutter was probably a fuel line blockage. We cleaned the system through and examined the fuel tanks for rust, that kind of thing, but we didn't find anything. We've tested the engines and they should be fine."

"And the power loss on the other plane?"

"We're not sure. We replaced some parts. There were a couple of things which looked as if they were worn, and there was some wiring loose that could have caused it. I suppose the connectors might have worked free, although it seems unlikely. Just bad luck, maybe?"

I exchanged a glance with Maria. Perhaps it was a coincidence after all.

"Thanks for sorting the problems out so quickly," I said.

"You're welcome, ma'am," Victoria said with a smile.

We saluted and returned to the rest of the squadron. "It all seems right and tight," I said. "We'll repeat yesterday's exercise. Let's get to it."

Maria and I were soon strapped in. I fired up the engines and we barrelled down the runway.

"Let's hope nothing else happens today," I said, pulling back on the stick to get us airborne.

"Amen to that."

In short order the flight was in formation. We were ready to go.

"Bluebirds, low-level, keep it tight. Here we go," I said.

Maria gave out the bearing. I dropped the kite down as low as I dared and opened up the throttle. We were away. Concerns about mechanical failures were forgotten as I focused on the task ahead.

"Hedge," said Maria.

"Got it."

"Poles."

"Seen them."

We made the first waypoint, and then the second. It was time to head back. We were skimming the ground over a long stretch of open field when suddenly the rudder pedals went loose.

"I've lost the rudder," I told Maria, trying not to panic.

"What?" She looked at me in alarm.

"The rudder — it's gone slack. I've lost it," I told her, thinking fast.

"Stay calm, for goodness' sake," she said.

"I am staying calm," I said.

"Not you, I was talking to myself," she said.

I couldn't help laughing, in spite of our predicament.

I pulled back on the stick and thankfully we began to gain height. It was only the rudder that was out of action.

"Bluebirds, I've got a problem," I said over the radio. "I've lost the rudder. I'm returning to base. Bluebird Four, take over the flight and continue the exercise."

However, Jennifer had other ideas. "Negative, Bluebird Leader, we'll escort you in. We're not leaving you to go back alone."

"Bluebird Four, I'm giving you an order," I said.

"And I'm not obeying it," Jennifer shot back.

I sighed and tried Patricia instead. "Bluebird Five," I said, "take over."

"Negative," said Patricia.

I swore under my breath in frustration.

Maria looked at me. "Let it go," she said. "What are you going to do, go through the entire squadron?"

"All right, fine, they win," I replied.

I spoke to the flight. "Bluebirds, stay with me. We are returning to base. I'm going to have to bank very wide to turn, so loosen up the formation."

"Roger," came the response, and the others moved away to give me room.

It wasn't easy, but I knew that flying without a rudder wasn't the end of the world. I still had the other controls. It just made turning more difficult.

"Control," I said as I began to line up an approach, "this is Bluebird Leader. I've lost my rudder. I'm coming in to land."

"Roger, Bluebird Leader, the runway is clear. Tenders will be on standby."

Once I had us square-on towards the runway, it was easy to take the Mosquito down without too much trouble.

"Now I know why I picked you," said Maria as the wheels touched the ground.

"Why is that?" I asked.

"Because you're a bloody good pilot."

"I'm glad you've finally noticed," I said with a grin.

We laughed with relief. I couldn't understand why the rudder had suddenly gone, but no doubt we'd find out soon enough.

As soon as I jumped down from the plane, I found myself confronted by Linda.

"Why the hell did you allow those pilots to disobey your orders?" she demanded.

I was taken aback by her anger, but she hadn't finished.

"You don't deserve that rank, Nightingale, you never did; you're a disgrace to the Air Force."

I usually shied away from conflict, but this time I fired up at once. "Oh, really? Well, you can take it up with the Wing Commander. In the meantime, stand to attention when I'm talking to you. I'm still the senior officer here," I told her.

"Well, *I'm* disobeying your order now — how about that?" Linda said, looking defiant.

Before I could say anything further, Jennifer intervened. She placed herself between us, facing Linda down.

"If you say one more word, officer or not, I swear to God I will —" She was cut off as a very loud new voice entered the fray.

"What is going on here?"

It was James, accompanied by Henry and Gloria. The entire squadron snapped to attention at once. I didn't know just how much he'd seen, but I was ashamed nonetheless.

"All right, break it up," James said in more even tones when he reached us. "When you get back to base, I want to see FO Nightingale, SO Nightingale and SO Harris in my office."

"Sir, I —" Linda began.

James held up his finger. "Not another word, Section Officer Harris. You can say all you want to me later." He nodded to Gloria.

"Right, ladies," she said. "Show's over. You're all dismissed. Get back to Hawberry."

The group broke up in silence.

"Thanks," I whispered to Jennifer.

"It's all right, but I think we're in trouble," she whispered back.

Everyone was getting into the trucks, and I was just about to join them when Victoria came up to me with a worried expression on her face.

"Ma'am, there's something I think you should see," she said.

"Can it wait?" I asked.

"No, ma'am," she said. "I really don't think it can."

"All right," I said. "Show me."

I accompanied her back to my Mosquito. The bomb bay doors were open, and she beckoned me underneath the plane with her.

"Look," she said, pointing up into the bomb bay.

"What am I looking at?" I asked, puzzled.

"The linkage to the rudder — it's been tampered with. We'll have to examine it more closely, but it looks like it's been cut."

I felt the blood drain from my face. Was someone trying to kill me?

"What? But then wouldn't it have failed right away?" I asked her.

"Not if it was only partially cut — then it might have worn through and snapped in mid-air," she replied.

"Which is exactly what happened," I said. I thought quickly. "Who knows about this?" I asked.

"Only me and a couple of the mechanics," she said.

"Tell nobody else. Keep this quiet. Can you take some photographs before you repair the damage? They may come in useful. We'll talk more about this later."

I left the Mosquito in a pensive mood, all thoughts of the fight with Linda forgotten. The plane had been deliberately sabotaged. What did that mean, and who could have done it? I would have to tell James.

As I jumped into the back of the truck, Jennifer patted the seat beside her.

"Saved you a place," she said.

"What did Victoria want?" Maria asked me.

"I'll tell you later. Got to deal with what just happened with Linda first," I told her.

"I'd like to deal with her all right," said Maria. "I'd like to knock her bl—"

"All right, let's settle down," I said. "I'm in enough trouble already."

"You're in trouble?" said Connie indignantly. "Linda bloody well started it."

"It's my fault," said Jennifer. "I disobeyed an order."

I squeezed her hand. "We've done worse, you and I. Remember when we bunked off school that time and Daddy was really angry?"

Jennifer laughed and the others immediately wanted to hear about it. It was a distraction from the impending interview with James. I wasn't looking forward to it.

CHAPTER SIXTEEN

Jennifer, Linda and I stood in front of the desk in James's office. James seemed unruffled, although he had spoken quite sharply when he had intervened in our argument.

"Perhaps one of you would like to tell me what occurred?" said James.

"I will," said Jennifer quickly before I could speak. "Anna's rudder failed, and she ordered me to take over the flight while she returned to base. I refused and insisted on escorting her home, sir."

"And why did you do that?"

"Because, sir, Anna is my sister and I was worried about her. I wasn't going to let her return alone, even if it meant disobeying an order."

"Being protective of your own is commendable," James said. "But what if this had been an actual mission?"

"Then I would have had to let her go, of course," said Jennifer, dropping her gaze.

"Right," he said, without further comment. "And I'm assuming that this event led to the altercation after the flight landed. Who started that?"

It felt as if we were back at school, explaining ourselves to the headmaster. I felt acutely embarrassed.

"I did, sir," said Linda. "I told FO Nightingale that she shouldn't have let the pilots disobey orders —"

Jennifer cut in. "SO Harris said a great deal more than that, sir. She said —"

"I don't want to hear it," James interrupted her firmly. "You know, when I formed this unit, this wasn't how I imagined it.

171

Officers arguing like schoolchildren about who should or shouldn't be in charge."

I knew perfectly well he had heard the exchange, but perhaps the exigencies of command dictated that he shouldn't comment upon it to us.

He paused and I saw disappointment in his face.

"I am aware, SO Harris, of your sentiments regarding my choice of Flight Leader," he continued. "But I let it go because I felt that you, and indeed all of you, would be adult enough to deal with it and act for the greater good of the Sirens."

Linda stared straight ahead, saying nothing.

"If you have a problem, SO Harris, you come to me. Is that clear?"

"Yes, sir," said Linda.

"I know what it takes to lead a flight in combat situations — what it takes to be a good leader. My decisions are not up for question," he continued.

"No, sir," said Linda.

"But it seems you *do* want to question them. So let me offer you a choice: would you prefer to return to the ATA and transport planes, or do you want to continue serving in the Sirens?"

There was silence. I saw Linda pale at his words. The CO really was prepared to throw her out if she didn't toe the line.

"I don't want to leave the Sirens, sir," Linda replied in a small voice.

James nodded. "Then see that nothing like this happens again," he told her. "You are dismissed, SO Harris."

Linda saluted and left the office. After she had gone, James let out a sigh.

"What am I to do with you two?" he said. "Jennifer, you know I could have you court-martialled for disobeying a direct order?"

"I'm ready to stand trial, sir, and defend my actions," Jennifer replied, unrepentant.

"Don't be ridiculous," he said with a laugh. "You're one of the best pilots I've got." He became serious again. "Plus, I can't afford to have it on record that anything is amiss with this unit. It would simply be taken as evidence by some that women cannot handle themselves in combat. You will make a public apology for your actions to the rest of the squadron and pledge to follow orders in future. I will not have insubordination in my squadron," he said firmly. "Understood?"

"Yes, sir," said Jennifer, swallowing hard. "Thank you, sir."

"You can go," he told her.

Jennifer saluted and left the room.

"Anna," said James, once she had gone. "You were in a difficult position, I know. It's difficult to enforce orders if people refuse to obey them. Particularly, I suppose, when one of those people is your sister."

"Yes, sir," I said.

"All right…" He hesitated and I jumped in. He had to know what Victoria had shown me.

"There is something else," I began.

"Go on."

"The rudder cable on my plane was cut deliberately; I'm pretty sure it was sabotage."

James suddenly looked very grim. "Have a seat, Anna. Tell me more."

Once I had finished, James became decisive. "I'm grounding the flight while we conduct an investigation. I will get MI6 down here. There's one obvious person we need to question first," he said.

"You don't mean Linda?" I said, aghast.

"Yes, I do mean Linda," he said. "I cannot afford to rule her out."

"If it's not her, then I'd like to help find the saboteur," I said.

"How?"

"Set a trap, something like that," I told him, thinking on my feet.

James laughed. "All right, keep this information close for the moment. We'll talk again once Linda has been questioned."

"Yes, sir."

"And Anna…" he said, smiling.

"Yes, sir?"

"Chin up."

I saluted and left the office, smiling to myself.

Naturally, I was waylaid by the usual gang as soon as I left James's office.

"Anna, what happened?"

"What did James say?"

I laughed at the questions. The one thing I couldn't tell them about, of course, was the investigation into the rudder cable.

"I'm still a Flight Officer," I told them instead.

"What about Linda? I really want to give her a piece of my mind," said Shelly.

"Please just let it go now — James has dealt with it."

"If you say so," said Shelly, not sounding at all mollified by my words.

"Agreed," said Maria. "Let's move on."

"To lunch?" said Patricia. "I'm starved."

A meeting was held directly after lunch. We assembled in the briefing room. I glanced across at Linda, sitting a couple of rows back, but she avoided my gaze. I wondered if she really had cut the cable to the rudder, and how anyone could go to those lengths just because they bore a grudge.

James, Henry and Gloria came in and took the podium. Once we were all seated, James spoke.

"In view of the fact that FO Nightingale's Mosquito rudder failed," he said, "I'm grounding the squadron until further notice."

It was a wise precaution, since we didn't know if mine was the only plane to have been sabotaged.

James paused, choosing his next words with care. "We are fighting a war," he said, "in case any of you have forgotten it. We are preparing for a difficult mission and all of your attention needs to be on that. Personal feelings have to be put aside for the greater good. We cannot afford to fail. People's lives, *your* lives, depend upon it. I have absolute faith in you to carry out your duty.

"We are doing something nobody in this country has done before. Putting women, yourselves, on the front line in combat against a formidable enemy. That achievement alone should be enough for anyone, regardless of their position in this squadron."

He was passionate, that much was clear. I thought about how his persistence had brought us all together, and how privileged we all were to be part of such an elite unit.

"All right," James said, "I believe Section Officer Jennifer Nightingale has something she would like to say."

I glanced at Jennifer, who had coloured up. Connie squeezed her hand as Jennifer stood up and walked to the podium. She stood looking at us all and spoke in a loud, clear voice.

"I would like to apologise," she said, "to Flight Officer Anna Nightingale for disobeying a direct order."

She looked at me as she said it and I smiled encouragingly.

"I also want to apologise for setting a poor example as an officer of this squadron. It was badly done and I'm sorry. I also pledge that I will never disobey an order again."

For a moment nobody spoke, and then Shelly stood up and shouted, "Three cheers for Jenny! Hip hip hooray…"

The room was filled with cheering for Jennifer. I saw tears in her eyes. As the cheering died down, Connie began a chant.

"Sirens, Sirens, Sirens…"

We all joined in, and for a full minute the entire squadron was standing and chanting our name with pride. James let it go on for a while and then called us all to order.

"All right, all right," he said, laughing. "Very good, bravo. That was a timely reminder of who we are, the Sirens, and don't ever forget it."

Everyone broke into spontaneous applause. Jennifer resumed her seat and Connie took her hand.

"So, as I said," James continued, "there will be no more flying for the moment. We will reconvene as soon as I have more news about the aircraft. Dismissed."

The following day, Judy sought me out.

"Could you come with me please, ma'am?" she said.

"Where are we going?" I asked her.

"I can't say," she replied.

I had to be satisfied with that until we arrived at our destination. It wasn't James's office, which surprised me. Instead, I was ushered into the same room in which James and I had eaten lunch. Seated in the easy chairs were the Marx Brothers.

"Ah, Flight Officer Nightingale," said Harpo, standing up to greet me, cigarette in hand.

"Hello," I said.

"Have a seat," said Chico.

I sat on the sofa and waited expectantly while Harpo took a drag on his cigarette. "We've been apprised of recent events," he said. "And we're here to help."

"All right," I replied, wondering what they wanted from me.

"We're going to interrogate SO Harris," said Chico. "And we want you to be present."

"What?" I said, slightly alarmed.

"We want you to listen in and observe the conversation, then give us your thoughts on it, if that's all right with you?"

"Yes, yes, of course," I said. "Whatever you need."

"That's the ticket," said Harpo.

"We knew you'd agree," said Chico.

"So, when is this interview going to take place?" I asked them.

"Oh, any moment now, once you're in position," said Chico.

"In position?" I must have looked slightly alarmed.

"The advantage of an old place like this is that it has some fortuitous features — such as a room which contains a secret hiding place from where you can observe proceedings without being seen."

I stared at him.

"Don't worry, we're not here to coerce SO Harris or anything like that. We're just going to ask her about the rudder cable and try to get to the truth."

"If indeed," added Harpo, "there is some truth to be found. We still don't know she did it."

"All right," I said. "Then I suppose we'd best get started."

"All in good time," said Chico.

177

I discovered that when they said immediately, that wasn't what they meant. Ambiguity seemed to be part of their makeup. They finished their cigarettes at leisure and lit up two more. They then smoked them while keeping up an entirely mundane conversation with me until they presumably felt ready.

"Right," said Harpo, slowly stubbing out his cigarette. "No sense in hanging around."

"No, indeed," said Chico, following suit.

I was beginning to learn that these two kept their own schedule.

The Marx Brothers led me along a couple of corridors and then into another, larger room with high ceilings. In the centre was a rather ornately decorated table with a leather top. There were two chairs on one side and one on the other.

Harpo crossed the room to what appeared to be part of the wainscoting and pressed it lightly. It swung open, revealing a small stairway.

"All rather secret squirrel stuff," said Chico, smiling.

"Up you go," said Harpo. "You'll find a small room with a chair. You will be able to see what goes on from there."

I entered the opening rather gingerly and climbed the staircase. It opened out into a room, just as they'd said.

"All right?" Chico called up to me.

"Yes, I'm fine," I said.

"Get yourself settled while we fetch Section Officer Harris."

A chair was placed next to an ornate filigree wooden screen. I could see the whole room through it. I saw that the pattern extended around the top part of the room and as such would not be noticeable unless you knew it was there. I sat down and waited.

Just then, the door opened and the Marx Brothers came into the room once more, accompanied by Linda.

"Have a seat, Section Officer Harris," said Harpo, indicating the single chair.

Linda sat down and the Marx Brothers sat opposite. The two of them lit up cigarettes after offering one to Linda. To my surprise, she took it. Perhaps she was feeling a little under pressure. From my vantage point I could see her clearly. They had placed her seat in such a way that I could note her expressions. She did not seem unduly fazed.

"Do you know why we want to talk to you?" said Harpo in a conversational manner.

"No," said Linda. "Unless it's about the other day, but I thought we'd already cleared that up with the Wing Commander."

"Indirectly … yes," said Chico.

"Meaning?" Linda took a drag on her cigarette.

Harpo took what appeared to be a photograph out of his pocket and placed it on the table. I remembered that I'd asked Victoria to take a picture of the rudder cable.

"Do you know what this is, Section Officer?" Harpo asked her.

Linda picked it up casually, then put it down again. "No, should I?" she said.

"That's the rudder cable taken from the bomb bay of Flying Officer Nightingale's Mosquito," said Harpo.

"And?"

Linda seemed a little belligerent and I wasn't sure why. Perhaps it was just her manner.

"Look at it again," suggested Chico, pushing the photo towards her. "What do you notice about the cable?"

Linda examined it more closely this time. She looked a little taken aback. "It looks as though it's been frayed or something — cut, maybe."

"Precisely," said Harpo.

"Bingo," said Chico.

Linda stared at them. "What are you suggesting?" she said. "Are you trying to say that I cut it? Is that what this is about?"

"Did you?" said Chico.

"What?"

"Did you cut the cable?" he repeated.

"No, of course I didn't cut it! What do you take me for?" Linda's fingers trembled as she put the cigarette into her mouth and took a puff, perhaps to steady her nerves.

"What do you think could have happened to Flight Officer Nightingale had it snapped at a less opportune moment?" asked Chico, changing tack.

"I don't know — I mean, there could have been a serious accident," said Linda.

"Exactly. Which amounts to attempted murder, doesn't it?" said Harpo. "So, we'll ask you once again, Section Officer, did you cut that cable?"

"No, I didn't cut the bloody cable. I wouldn't do that!" she shouted.

"It's no secret that you don't like Flight Officer Nightingale, is it?" said Chico, taking a softer tone.

Linda sighed. "I wouldn't say I don't like her... I was perhaps jealous of her. Of her position."

"So if, say, she was no longer in the squadron, then the position of Flight Leader might once more be vacant, yes?" asked Harpo.

"Well, yes, but I'm not going to murder a colleague just to get her job," said Linda.

"So you say," said Chico.

"I do say, because I didn't do it!" Linda shot back at him.

"You had the motive, the means and no doubt the opportunity," said Harpo, ignoring her denial.

I almost felt sorry for Linda, with the way the Marx Brothers were harrying her.

"I keep telling you that I did not cut that cable. I'm not mechanically minded. Ask anyone. I couldn't even mend my bicycle when the chain came off it."

For quite some time, Chico and Harpo said nothing more but instead sat smoking their cigarettes and completing unnerving her.

"Why don't you like Flight Officer Nightingale?" said Harpo, changing tack.

I sat forward, interested to hear more.

"I … I didn't say I didn't like her, as such," said Linda.

"Well, you obviously don't like her, do you? You attempted to undermine her position as Flight Leader. That's not something you do to someone you like, now, is it?" said Chico.

Linda sighed. "All right, fine. I don't like her because she comes from money, and the opportunities just seem to fall into her lap. I've had to work hard for everything I've got. What has she done to deserve her position?"

Harpo took a drag on his cigarette and stubbed it out in an ashtray. He immediately lit up another. He offered one to Linda, but this time she declined it.

"You don't know much about the Nightingale sisters, do you?" said Chico. "They don't come from money; they're farm girls from Sussex. They also happen to have years of experience as stunt pilots in their father's flying circus. We have it on good authority that they are two of the best pilots we've ever recruited."

Linda looked surprised. "I may have been a little quick to form an opinion, then," she conceded.

Harpo glanced at his colleague and then back at Linda. "You can go," he said.

"What?"

"You're free to go."

"Then you believe me? You don't think I cut the cable?"

"No, we don't, but we had to be sure," said Chico.

"However, if you hear anything about who it might have been, then make sure you inform us as once. And another thing — nothing we've discussed leaves this room," said Harpo.

"Strictly on the QT," said Chico. "All right?"

"Yes, yes, I won't tell a soul," said Linda, getting up.

"Toodle pip," said Harpo.

Linda left the room looking immensely relieved. As soon as she had gone, Harpo came to the bottom of the stairs and called up to me.

"You can come down now," he said. "The coast is clear."

I made my way back into the room. Harpo indicated more comfortable seating and we all sat down.

"Well?" he said. "What did you think? Was she telling the truth?"

"I think she was, yes," I said.

"We think so too," said Chico.

"We've got a nose for it ... lying, that is," Harpo added.

I realised why Linda hadn't been chosen to lead the flight, even if she couldn't see it herself. She was far too quick to anger and if I knew one thing, it was that a leader needed a level head. But that didn't make her a liar.

"Anyway," Chico continued, "if the saboteur is not SO Harris, then who is it?"

I took a deep breath. I'd been thinking about this while the scene had been playing out earlier. "I don't know who it is, but I would like to help find out," I said, "if you'll let me. I have a plan, and it will involve one or two of my colleagues."

"Go on," said Chico.

"We're all ears," said Harpo.

I outlined the bones of my idea while they listened patiently. A little while later, having secured their agreement, I left the room and went to round up the others.

CHAPTER SEVENTEEN

My room became our secret HQ. Present were myself, Jennifer, Maria, Shelly, Patricia, and Connie. I also had to involve Susan and Pamela, because it would be hard to exclude them. They'd become part of our little group.

Before I spoke, I locked the door. This drew some surprised looks from the others.

"What I'm about to tell you is top secret," I said. "It can go no further than us, understood?"

When they nodded their assent, I told them about the saboteur while they listened in astonishment. Once they had heard what had happened, there was immediate outrage.

Maria jumped up from the bed and declared, "I don't care what she said to the Marx Brothers, I reckon it's Linda."

"Hush!" I admonished her. "Not so loud. Anyway, I don't think it is Linda. It must be someone else."

"But who?" asked Connie, who was sitting by the window next to Jennifer.

There was silence for a moment, and then Shelly snapped her fingers.

"Gary! I bet it's bloody Gary!" she said fiercely. "He has access to the planes and may be looking for revenge after what we did to him."

"Yes!" said Patricia. "Let's go and confront him right now!"

I held up my hands to halt their impetuousness.

"All right, stop!" I told them firmly, wondering if I'd made a mistake taking them into my confidence. "I have a plan. But we're doing it my way or we're not doing it at all."

"Let the woman speak," Maria put in, lending me her support.

"Go on then, tell us your plan," said Jennifer.

"All right, listen. Yes, I think Gary could be a suspect, but if it turns out that he's not responsible, then we have to find out who is."

"And how do we do that?" said Patricia.

I outlined my plan without further interruption. When I had finished, I sat back and waited. No one spoke.

"Well?" I said at length.

"I think it's a good plan," said Maria. "When are we going to do it?"

"First, I have to run it by James, and then we'll see."

"The sooner the better, surely," Connie suggested.

"Yes," I agreed. "You're right. I'll speak to him first thing."

I went to find James directly after breakfast the following day. He was in his office when I knocked and entered.

"Anna," he said, smiling. "What can I do for you?"

"James," I said without thinking and then corrected myself at once, blushing furiously. "I mean, sir…"

"I much prefer James," he said affably. "There's nobody around for us to be concerned about protocol."

"James … I would like to go over my plan to catch the saboteur."

"The MI6 chaps said you'd be coming to talk to me, so I was rather expecting it."

"I've been discussing it with the others…"

"And who are the others?" he asked.

I told him and he nodded. "Tell me the whole," he said.

"Here's my idea," I said, and explained how we intended to lay a trap, after we'd questioned Gary and assuming it wasn't him.

"Why not just let MI6 interrogate Gary?" James asked.

"Because I think he'll be more truthful if we do it," I said.

"And why is that?"

"Because he's afraid of us after what we did last time," I said, smiling.

"Anna, on no account are you to attempt to drop him out of a plane again," James told me sternly, though his tone was tinged with amusement.

"Of course not, but we might *threaten* to do it," I replied mischievously. "And if it's not him, are you happy with Plan B?" I asked.

"Yes, indeed, but there is one thing…"

I watched curiously as James opened one of his desk drawers. He carefully placed two pistols on the desktop and a box of ammunition. I stared at them in surprise.

"I want you to take these," he said. "It could be dangerous. I don't want you going unarmed."

"All right," I said, taking the guns and putting one in each pocket.

"I want them back afterwards," he said, in case I had other ideas.

"Yes, of course."

We had sidearms which we took into the planes with us. They were service revolvers, but these were far neater and unobtrusive.

"Don't hesitate to use them," James continued, "if you find yourself in a situation where you need to."

This impressed upon me the possibility that we might actually be in danger. It didn't deter me from the course of action, however.

"I'm only allowing this escapade because I trust you implicitly and that motley crew you've assembled to carry out the plan."

"I'm flattered you think so highly of me," I said and then immediately regretted it.

"I think more highly of you than you know, Anna."

I blushed at his words. "I'd better get on then," I said hastily, almost fleeing from his office with unseemly haste. "I'll keep you informed."

Outside in the corridor I tried to still my beating heart. Judy passed by at that inopportune moment.

"Are you all right, ma'am?" she asked me. "You seem a little flustered."

"Yes, I'm fine, just … you know." I hurried away, leaving her staring after me.

When I entered my room, I discovered that the others had been waiting for me with ill-concealed impatience.

"Well?" Shelly asked.

"We are Condition Green," I told them. "And I've got these."

I took the two pistols out of my pockets and laid them on the bed.

"Now you're talking," said Maria, eyeing them with satisfaction.

Questioning Gary had to wait. That afternoon it was time for the funeral of ASO Frances York. I carefully hid the pistols and ammunition in our room and then Jennifer and I put on our well pressed number one uniforms along with the rest of the Sirens.

Frances's coffin was processed from the Hall to the chapel in the grounds. It was placed on a gun carriage for the purpose and covered by the Union Jack. The Sirens led the procession with me at the front. James, Henry and Gloria followed the coffin along with the Frances's family. Other RAF and WAAF personnel followed them. Sergeant Wallace gave us all the funeral parade orders.

Unusually for the WAAF we had been issued with rifles for the occasion. James didn't subscribe to the normal protocols. We'd all been trained in the use of firearms, including rifle drill. For the funeral procession, the rifles were carried in the crook of the left arm with the butt pointing upwards and the barrel pointing behind us to the ground.

The squadron chaplain walked in front of the procession dressed in uniform but wearing the traditional dog collar of a priest.

"Funeral Parade, forward march!" came the order from Sergeant Wallace when we were all assembled.

We processed to the chapel in silence. I felt choked up knowing that Frances had died on my watch. Deep down, I knew that she would not be the last.

When we arrived at the chapel, Sergeant Wallace said, "Guard of Honour form up!" and then, "Present arms!"

We stood on either side of the path up to the chapel entrance, presenting our rifles in salute. The coffin was carried up the path and inside for the service. It was followed in by the family and then by us. It seemed odd to be seated in the chapel with rifles, but we were at war, after all.

"We are gathered here to mourn the tragic loss of Assistant Section Officer Frances York," said the chaplain, "who died in the performance of her duty transporting planes to airfields around the country."

I glanced at Maria and the others. There were a few wry smiles. The chaplain was sticking closely to the script.

"An unfortunate and unforeseen accident has taken her from us and from her family, far too soon. Frances was…"

He began to talk of Frances's life. How many more unfortunate accidents would this squadron have as we rolled into the missions? Wouldn't people become suspicious? No doubt James had a plan for that too. The other problem was that there might not be a body next time. The next person to die might be left on enemy soil in a burnt-out plane, or even lost in the Channel.

As the chaplain spoke on, I pushed the thoughts away. We had more pressing issues to resolve than possible future deaths.

Frances's father and then her brother talked in moving terms about her. I tried not to picture my father and mother standing up there doing the same for me or Jennifer. I fought back my tears at the thought. I felt it would not be seemly to cry overtly.

James stood up and took the podium.

"Thank you all for coming," he said. "I can't add too much to what has been said. However, never let it be imagined that Frances was not courageous, for that she was. Every person in this squadron is as dedicated to the cause of fighting this war as any other service man or woman in this country. They all serve in their way. We are grateful for their service. We are grateful for Frances's service and sorry that it ended this way."

All of us knew what he was saying underneath those words. Nobody but the few who served in the Sirens would ever know she had died in combat and that was a shame.

Unexpectedly, James then said, "If she would like to, I invite Flight Officer Anna Nightingale, the Flight Leader of the Sirens to say a few words."

My head jerked up at this. He had taken me by surprise. All eyes turned to me. I had no choice but to stand up. Would I like to, indeed! I walked to the podium, a little angry at James for putting me on the spot. He gave way to me and I shot him a dagger-filled glance, then turned to speak.

"I just want to say…" I began. Everyone waited expectantly while I hesitated. What did I want to say? What could I say? I didn't even know Frances that well. "I just want to say," I repeated, recovering my composure, "that all of us in the squadron deeply mourn the loss of Frances. We are all here, as Wing Commander Donnington has said, to do our bit for the war. Frances certainly did that. She was a trooper in every way. We … all of us … will miss her very much. Thank you."

I looked at James and he gave me a brief nod of approval. I smiled at him, my annoyance temporarily forgotten, and returned to my seat. Maria squeezed my hand as I resumed my place next to her.

"Now," said the chaplain, "the coffin will proceed to the graveside, where I will administer the last rites."

"Escort Party take your positions," said Sergeant Wallace.

That was us. We stood up and formed two columns in front of the coffin. It was processed out of the chapel and into the graveyard. The flag was removed, folded and handed to a family member. The coffin was then lowered into the grave.

James had decided that we would fire a gun salute over the coffin. Again, this was something which very possibly went against protocol. However, there wasn't anyone to stop him. We all felt it was most appropriate.

"Firing party, forward!" said Sergeant Wallace.

Six of the Sirens, including Maria, Connie and Carol, took up their places at the graveside.

Six salvos were fired into the air as Sergeant Wallace said, "Reload, fire…" over and over again.

Once done, the chaplain gave the traditional last rights ending with, "Ashes to ashes, dust to dust…"

I glanced around at the other Sirens. There were not many dry eyes after all as we said our final goodbye to our colleague.

Following the ceremony, we came together for the wake in the dining room, where refreshments were served. We all attended. I wondered if this would be the norm for squadron fatalities or whether this was just because it was our first.

James came up to me as I was standing on my own drinking a cup of tea.

"I … er … I'm sorry that I sprung that on you," he said with a tentative smile, referring to the impromptu speech in the chapel.

"I was rather cross with you," I shot at him without thinking. At once I regretted assuming such familiarity.

"I hope you're not still cross then?" he said, putting on the most endearing grin.

"No, I think I can forgive you," I told him, smiling back.

"Thank goodness for that," he said, sounding completely unabashed.

"It was a good ceremony, was it not?" I said.

"Fitting, yes," he said.

"What if…" I paused.

"If it happens again, or they don't come back?" he finished for me.

"Yes," I said.

"We'll still hold a funeral, regardless," he replied. "This isn't just because it's the first time, if that's what you're wondering. You are all deserving of a good send-off if it comes to it."

"It will happen again, won't it?" I said without thinking.

"Yes, I'm afraid it's all to likely, Anna, but I hope … not to you."

Before I could answer, he excused himself to talk to Frances's family. Perhaps he felt he had revealed too much of himself.

"And what were you and James talking about?" said Maria, sidling up to me unnoticed.

"Why?"

"Because you're blushing."

"Oh!" I put a hand to my face as if to cover it. "Well … you know … just…"

I didn't finish and she shot me a knowing look. A look which said, *There's more to you two than meets the eye.*

With the funeral over with, our next port of call was Gary. I gathered my band together and we cadged a lift to the airfield in a truck. Nothing else was happening that afternoon, so it seemed quite opportune. Some discussion was had about who would have the pistols. In end I gave one to Maria and kept one for myself, partly because she seemed more than eager to have one.

"You have to give it back when this is all sorted," I informed her.

"If I must…" she said.

"You must."

"Fine, then."

She sighed dramatically and rolled her eyes. I laughed. We had come up with a plan to lure Gary out of the hangar to confront him.

"Why do I have to be the bait?" Shelly protested when she was picked for the task.

"Because he knows you, he won't suspect," Connie told her.

"All right, but you owe me," Shelly said, aggrieved. "I wasn't ever going near him again."

"As if you've ever kept *that* promise before," Maria said sarcastically.

"There's always a first time," Shelly said with a mock pout.

When we arrived at the airfield, we alighted from the back of the truck. On the pretext of inspecting something, I led the others around the side of the hangar while Shelly sauntered inside.

A few moments later she appeared with the unsuspecting Gary in tow. As soon as he saw us, he stopped dead and turned as if to run. Maria was quicker.

"Not so fast," she said, levelling the pistol at his chest.

He stared at it as if he couldn't believe his eyes. It was the second time we'd had him at pistol point.

"What the hell are you people doing?" he demanded. Then he rounded on Shelly. "You told me you wanted to have a chat, for old times' sake. What's going on?"

"We are going to have a chat, only not just the two of us," said Shelly, amused.

"But I thought…" He trailed off.

She looked at him with mild contempt. "You thought what, Gary? That I would ever touch you again after what you did? No chance."

"Look, I don't know what you women are playing at," said Gary, turning his attention to us, "but I didn't do it!"

"What didn't you do, Gary?" asked Connie, moving in a little closer.

"I … I don't know, whatever I'm supposed to have done that you … b-bloody women are giving me trouble about," he replied.

"What do you *think* you've done?" said Patricia, joining in.

"Yes, Gary!" said Pamela. "Tell us."

He looked from one to the other of us, completely perplexed.

"You're bloody mad, the lot of you. There's something seriously wrong with you. You've all got a bloody screw loose, I swear," he said.

"You'll have more than a screw loose if you don't own up to it," said Maria in threatening tones.

"Own up to what?" he said in despair. "You're crazy."

Realising this wasn't getting us anywhere, I decided to intervene. I motioned to them to give me some space, but Maria didn't drop her aim.

"Gary," I said, "I'm going to ask you something, and you had better tell the truth. If you don't, then perhaps we need to take another trip in the B-17."

He paled at my words and looked extremely apprehensive. "Go on…" he said.

"The rudder cable on my Mosquito was cut," I told him.

He regarded me aghast. "What?"

"Did you do it?"

"What?" he repeated, as if unable to believe his ears.

"She said, did you bloody do it, you traitor," Maria put in forcefully.

"I didn't even know the cable had been cut," he said.

"Yeah, right," snorted Connie. "You're a mechanic. You work there — how could you not know that?"

"Because I don't work on all of the planes, and Victoria doesn't tell us everything. I just do my job and that's it. Nothing else."

I regarded him for a moment. I remembered how the Marx Brothers had been with Linda and decided to try and emulate their tactics.

"I'm not sure I believe you," I said. "I'm going to ask you again. Did you cut it?"

"What?" he said, looking at me as if he'd seen a ghost.

"Answer the question!" said Maria, who seemed to have adopted the role of my henchwoman.

"I did just answer it, for Christ's sake. I told you that I didn't do it and I didn't even know about it!" he said again.

"Should we beat him with a stick?" said Pamela suddenly. "I can go and find a suitable one. He'll soon talk."

"What … no! What's the matter with you?" said Gary, sounding alarmed. "You're like a coven of bloody witches."

"Nobody is beating anyone with sticks!" I said to Pamela, giving her a quelling look.

She shrugged. "It was just an idea."

"Gary," I said again. "I really want to believe you're telling us the truth. So, *are* you telling the truth?"

"I swear on my life, my mother's life, any life you want," he said. "I'm not lying."

I held his gaze. Although I didn't think I was a great judge of character with my limited experience of life, the look he gave me seemed to speak volumes.

"All right," I said. "I believe you."

He sighed with relief.

"You didn't know anything about the cable? You're sure?" I continued.

"No, nothing, honest. Can I go now, please?" he pleaded.

"All in good time," I said. "Firstly, you are not to tell anyone about the cable. If you do, we'll be back."

"You can bet your life on that," said Maria, still brandishing the gun.

"And secondly, keep your ear to the ground. If you hear anything, even a whisper, you come and tell us, all right?"

"Yes, yes, of course, got it, absolutely." He nodded vigorously. I could see he was chafing to get away.

"Promise?" I pressed.

"I swear," he said eagerly.

"Fine then. You can go," I said.

Maria lowered the gun and he took off like a rocket.

"Look at him run," said Shelly. "Always knew he was a coward at heart."

"Of course you did," said Maria in disbelieving tones.

"'Should we beat him with a stick?'" said Jennifer, bursting out laughing. "Pamela, honestly, what are you like?"

"You should have seen his face," said Patricia.

"Oh, I did."

We all collapsed with mirth for quite a while. I wondered if poor Gary could hear us. Once we had recovered, Jennifer spoke again.

"We're no further forward really, though, are we?"

"No," I said. "So now we go to Plan B."

Plan B involved some subterfuge and a little bit of cooperation. James had already agreed to it and so all that was necessary was to tell him we wanted to carry it out.

"We need to do what we discussed," I told him, sitting in front of his desk in his office.

"Sure," he said. "When would you like to set your trap?"

"I think if you announce the resumption of flying for the day after tomorrow, then we'll lie in wait in the hangar that evening, once the mechanics have all gone."

"All right," he said. "You're on…" He hesitated. "Are you sure you've got enough firearms?"

I laughed. "I'm sure the others would say no, but I think we probably have."

He opened another drawer and produced two more pistols, placing them on the desk. "Take these," he said.

"Have you got a whole armoury in there or what?" I asked with interest.

"I … just keep a few guns around in case, not just for me but for the others," he told me.

"In case of what?" I couldn't imagine why he'd need one pistol, let alone four.

He sighed. "This unit is potentially a prime target, should word get out to the enemy. You never know what could happen. So, I like to be prepared."

I stared at him, open-mouthed. "What? You're saying we could be attacked by … spies or something?"

He spread his arms wide as if in an apology. "Something like that, yes."

"Thanks for telling us before we joined up," I said sarcastically.

"Would it have stopped you from joining up?" he asked, raising an eyebrow and thus rendering me even more attracted to him than I already was.

"Well, no, but you could at least have said you thought we were in danger. It's nice to know we might be killed in our beds."

"I honestly don't think anything like that would happen, and if I did, then I'd issue firearms to all of you."

"Are you sure you're not just fond of collecting weapons?" I said, unable to prevent a teasing tone creeping into my voice.

"Now, that would be telling," he said. "I'll stick to my original excuse."

I shook my head. He was slowly sliding under all the defences I had put up against him.

"I know," he continued, noting my gesture. "I'm a lost cause."

"Yes, well," I said, coming to my senses. "I'll be off then, sir, and thank you for these additional pistols. All will be returned in good order."

"You know," he said, "I much preferred it just now, when you weren't quite so formal…"

"That's as it may be," I said, saluting smartly and turning on my heel.

"Dismissed, Flight Officer Nightingale," he said with a light laugh.

As I left the office, I found myself wondering whether we'd just been engaging in banter or flirting. I didn't know. I cursed myself for not being wiser in these matters, unlike Jennifer, who was thoroughly versed in the ways of the opposite sex. I just knew that he disconcerted me an awful lot, which for some reason I didn't find the least unpleasant. In fact, I rather liked it.

I entered my room and found the rest of my co-conspirators waiting for the verdict.

"Well?" said Jennifer, when I said nothing and stood there smiling instead.

"Well," I said, "Plan B begins tomorrow, and even better than that, Christmas has come early."

I took the two extra pistols out of my pockets and placed them on the bed.

"Oh, my giddy aunt," said Connie.

"I bagsy one of those," Patricia said at once.

"All right, ladies, don't fight over the pistols," I told them. "We can decide who has them in a civilised manner."

"What? A duel?" Pamela asked.

"No!" I said firmly. "We'll draw straws or something to make it fair."

"But where did you get these?" said Maria, picking one of them up.

"From James," I said.

"Why has he got four pistols?" Susan asked me.

"I … don't really know. Maybe he likes guns." I shrugged.

"Well, I don't care why he's got them," said Connie. "I'm going to get some straws."

CHAPTER EIGHTEEN

The following morning after breakfast, James held a briefing. He was as good as his word as he stood up on the podium with Henry and Gloria.

"I've decided to resume flying practice tomorrow morning," he said. "The planes have all been thoroughly checked and the technical crew are satisfied they're in working order."

He paused and I glanced around to gauge reactions. I couldn't see anything untoward. I assumed that if it was someone in our squadron, they wouldn't be silly enough to give themselves away. I really couldn't imagine why it would be one of us, though. It didn't make any sense.

"The forthcoming mission is too important to delay things any longer," he said. "We have to be fully prepared when the time comes to act with deadly decisiveness. This prison camp must be destroyed at all costs."

Once again, I took a quick look around the room. Everyone seemed intent on listening to what James had to say.

"The practice will begin directly after breakfast tomorrow," he said. "Unless there are any questions, you can carry on with your duties for today."

He dismissed us and we had nothing further to do but wait. There were no classes or drill that day. It seemed to drag quite a bit but finally, after dinner, it was time to go. I gathered the others once more in my room.

"All right," I said. "You all know what to do."

Everyone gave their assent. We drew straws and it fell to Jennifer, Shelly, Patricia and Pamela to be the firearms section of our team, much to Maria's disgust. However, she took it in good part since she'd already had a go with a pistol when we'd questioned Gary.

The truck drivers drove down to pick up the maintenance crews, and we hitched a ride in the back. It was starting to get dark by the time we arrived at the airfield. Once there, we moved into the shadows away from the hangar and out of sight.

Victoria came over and found me, since she was in on the scheme.

"Hi," she said. "There's nobody in the hangars, I've made sure of that. Just let yourselves in. And good luck."

"Thanks."

On that parting note, she left us and jogged over to one of the waiting trucks. She jumped into the front and the truck set off. Once it had disappeared, I turned to the others.

"All right," I said in a low voice. "Let's get in position."

"What if they don't come tonight?" said Shelly.

"Then we'll do it again, tomorrow," Maria told her. "Stop asking stupid questions."

"Look," I said, "if they already sabotaged the planes twice, the chances are very high they'll do it again, so let's just get on with it."

"Yes, come on," said Maria, following me as I set off at a rapid pace to the hangar. There was a small door set in the main door. I opened it, we all went inside and then I closed it. Apparently, the door wasn't locked but there was a regular jeep patrol which came by every so often and toured the airfield to check all was in order.

Once in the hangar, I said, "Everyone to your places, as agreed."

I had scouted the hangar out beforehand and ascertained the best places to hide. We split into two groups with two pistols each. There were some big wooden boxes and barrels strategically placed at the sides of the hangar. Inside what seemed quite a vast space stood all the Mosquitos. They had been wheeled quite close to each other so as not to take up too much room. Victoria had thoughtfully placed some blankets and boxes to sit on in our concealed positions.

We made ourselves comfortable and settled down to wait. I was with Maria, Shelly and Patricia, hiding behind a large stack of oil drums. Jennifer was with Susan, Connie and Pamela on the other side of the hangar behind some boxes.

"What do we do now?" whispered Shelly.

"Shut up and wait," Maria whispered back.

"God, how boring."

"This isn't for your entertainment," Maria told her. "It's for a serious purpose."

"I know, but I wish I'd brought some cards or something."

"God preserve us," Maria hissed, exasperated.

"Stop it, you two," I said.

"Yes, Boss," said Shelly.

"And stop calling me Boss."

"Yes, Boss."

Patricia had said nothing throughout this exchange and just rolled her eyes. Shelly was impossible sometimes and so I didn't rise to the bait. Instead, I sat on one of the boxes provided and pulled a blanket around me because it was rather cold. The others followed suit. We had been issued with greatcoats, and I wished I had brought one with me.

There was plenty of time to think while we waited. I wondered if the person would come and who it might be. I couldn't imagine why someone would sabotage our planes and endanger our mission. It didn't make any sense. If they were a spy, then surely telling the Germans where we were so they could carry out a bombing raid would be far more logical.

As my thoughts drifted from this to that, I noticed Shelly's eyelids drooping. I looked at my watch. It hadn't been all that long. I was debating with myself how long we should stay waiting for someone to show up when there was a creak from the access door.

Maria came alert at once and gave Shelly a nudge. Shelly drew her pistol and so did Patricia. There were soft footsteps echoing through the stillness of the hangar. We all exchanged looks while I motioned them to stay quiet. As we listened, the footsteps indicated a person moving around the planes. Still, I waited, wanting to find out what they would do. Then came the distinctive clang of the bomb bay doors on a plane falling open. It was time to act.

Cautiously I peered around the barrels. Three planes down there was a figure in the shadows underneath one of the Mosquitos. I looked over at the boxes on the other side and I could see Jennifer. I motioned to her to move in.

Very quietly we left our positions of cover. Then carefully and slowly, we advanced on the plane. As we got closer, the figure resolved into a female in uniform, but we still couldn't see her face. She was reaching up into the bomb bay, fiddling with something. I motioned to everyone to fan out. The woman was so intent on what she was doing that she didn't see or hear us as we surrounded her. At my signal, pistols were levelled. Then I stepped forward.

"Stop what you're doing," I said in a loud, clear voice. "You're under arrest."

The woman let out a gasp and dropped something. It clattered to the floor. She looked wildly left and right, perhaps thinking she could run, but realised she was trapped.

"Come out with your hands up," I said. "Show yourself."

"Yes, don't try to run or we'll gun you down," added Pamela.

"For goodness' sake," hissed Maria. "This isn't the movies."

I stifled a giggle in spite of the serious situation. The woman seemed hesitant to come out, so I tried again.

"You there, step out now," I said, motioning the others to move closer.

With some reluctance, the woman put her hands up and stepped forward, out of the shadows. Now we could finally see her.

"Ruth?" said Susan, staring at her.

It was Section Officer Ruth Maddison. I could hardly believe it.

"It's not what you're thinking," said Ruth.

"I'm pretty sure it's exactly what we're all thinking," I told her. "You're here to sabotage the planes."

Ruth shot me a stricken look. "No … I mean, yes … but I'm not a traitor … it's…" She burst into tears.

We looked at one another. This wasn't what we'd thought would happen. Instead of the expected defiance of a saboteur spy, we had one of our colleagues crying in front of us.

Susan glanced at me and then went over to Ruth. She put her arms around her. Ruth began to sob into Susan's jacket.

"It's all right, Ruth," she said. "It's all right."

"It very much is not all right," put in Patricia. "She's been tampering with the planes."

"She's still my friend," Susan shot back.

"Friend or not," I told her, taking charge, "she needs to be taken into custody and questioned properly. Also, can someone get that thing she dropped?"

"I will," said Connie, ducking under the plane to retrieve it.

I went over to Susan and Ruth, who seemed to be recovering her composure.

"You're being arrested for suspected sabotage by my authority as Flight Leader," I told her. "We're going to take you back to Hawberry; don't try to run or escape. We're armed and we won't hesitate to use our pistols."

I sounded more confident than I felt. Jennifer smiled at me in approval.

"Damn right," Pamela added.

"Don't worry, I'm not going to run," said Ruth. "Where could I go, in any case?"

The rest of the group surrounded Ruth as an escort.

"Here," said Connie, handing me a small pair of wire cutters. "This is what she dropped."

I put them in my pocket, intending to give them to James later as evidence. When we were all ready, I gave the order. "Let's go."

CHAPTER NINETEEN

The following morning, I sat at the side of the room the Marx Brothers had used to interrogate Linda. This time it was Ruth, and I was not in the hidey-hole. They had invited me to observe the questioning.

It had been an eventful night. Ruth had been secretly taken into custody and locked up in a room away from everyone else, under guard. None of us had really spoken to her after I'd arrested her. We were all shocked that she was responsible for sabotaging the planes. However, I didn't want the rest of the squadron to know anything, at least until we knew more about Ruth's motives.

Once she was safely out of the way and incarcerated, I ordered the others to keep quiet about what had happened, to which they reluctantly agreed. Pamela was particularly incensed.

"Her perfidy needs to be exposed," she said heatedly. "Ruth put your life in danger."

"We don't know why she did it," I told her. "At the very least I want to hear her explanation. Besides, it's up to James what action is taken."

Pamela was still fired up. "I know what I'd *like* to do."

"Yes, well, it's not your call to make. Also, you can all return the pistols to me, now that the show's over," I replied firmly.

The pistols having been surrendered, I took them back to James. Since it was late, he said very little but congratulated me and told me that we should await the results of Ruth's interrogation, as I had suggested.

Ruth was sitting on one side of the table, the Marx Brothers on the other, in what was obviously a familiar pattern for interrogation. The two spies were in no hurry to begin but instead lit up cigarettes and sat smoking them without saying anything. Ruth declined a cigarette and watched them nervously. She was a good-looking woman with curly brown hair and a fair complexion. Up until now, she had seemed to be a model pilot.

At length, Harpo knocked some ash off his cigarette into the ashtray. "Let's start at the beginning, shall we?" he said, pleasantly enough. "Were you responsible for the engine problems recently?"

"Yes," said Ruth without preamble. She must have realised that now she'd been caught, there wouldn't be any point in her lying.

"And the rudder cable?" asked Chico.

"Yes, that too."

Chico took a drag on his cigarette. The smoke caught in the rays of light coming through the window. It reminded me of a detective film I'd seen recently.

"And what were your intentions last night?" said Harpo. He placed the small pair of wire cutters we had retrieved from the hangar on the table. "I assume these are yours?"

Ruth nodded and said, "The same, I suppose. Just to loosen something so it would stop them flying."

"Just to loosen something…" Harpo trailed off for a moment, surveying her critically. "You realise that Flight Officer Nightingale might have been killed as a result of your tampering with the rudder cable?"

Ruth dropped her eyes. "I know that now," she said quietly. "That wasn't my intention."

"And what was your intention exactly, Section Officer?" said Chico with a hint of steel.

"To stop them flying, I told you … and I didn't even know it was Flight Officer Nightingale's plane. I just picked one at random."

"You picked one at random, you say, only because you wanted to ground the flight?" said Harpo in disbelief. "You must think we were born yesterday."

"Who are you working for?" said Chico suddenly.

Ruth looked up at him, startled by his tone. "What?"

"I said, who … are … you … working … for!" said Chico again, this time slamming his hand down on the desk after each word for emphasis.

Ruth looked alarmed at these tactics. "I'm not working for anybody. I don't know what you're talking about," she protested. Her voice became a little high-pitched and she seemed very scared.

"Pardon us if we don't believe you," said Harpo.

"Is it the Germans?" Chico shot at her.

"What? No! I'm not working for anybody. I told you … I'm not … I'm not," said Ruth desperately.

Harpo and Chico subsided for a moment. They finished their cigarettes, then immediately lit up two more. Harpo took a long drag before speaking again.

"You know the penalty for treason, don't you?" he said casually.

Ruth blenched visibly at his words.

"Hanging," said Chico. "Or being shot."

"Either way, it's death," said Harpo.

Ruth looked down miserably and a solitary tear trickled down her face.

"So, you see," Harpo continued, "it's curtains for you unless you start talking and tell us who put you up to this. We want names."

"There isn't anybody else," said Ruth in a small voice. "Just me. I did it. You can hang me if you must…"

For the first time, I saw exasperation in Harpo's face. The Marx Brothers were usually so laconic, but it seemed as if Ruth had them stumped. He and Chico stood up and motioned to me to leave the room.

"We'll be back," he informed Ruth as they accompanied me.

Outside in the corridor, Harpo turned to me and spoke in a low voice.

"She's got us a little at point non plus," he confessed. "It's not the usual way these things go when someone is a spy."

"Of course, we could try more forceful methods," suggested Chico.

I winced inwardly at the idea of this. Surely Ruth didn't deserve that?

"Do you think she's a spy?" I asked them. "I didn't get that impression, but I don't know much about spies."

"We can usually tell," said Harpo. "Quite quickly."

"I'd rather you didn't use more forceful methods," I said.

"Then why don't you talk to her?" Chico suggested.

"Me?"

"Yes, you. She might relate to you better than us. After all, you're a pilot, and she's a pilot."

I thought about it for a moment. The last thing I wanted was for Ruth to be tortured or coerced in some way.

"All right," I said. "But I'll talk to her my way…"

"Of course, we'll keep silent," said Harpo.

"As the grave," Chico added.

We re-entered the room. Ruth looked up in surprise when I took a seat across the table from her. The Marx Brothers went and sat at the far end near the window, out of her direct line of sight.

"Ruth," I said gently, "can I speak to you for a little while? Will that be all right?"

"Yes," she said, nodding.

I took the plunge. "Why did you do it, Ruth? Why did you sabotage the planes?"

She said nothing for a long while, so I tried again.

"We don't really know each other, Ruth. But I know you're a good pilot. To do something like this … you must have had a reason?"

She sighed. "What's the point of me explaining? They said I'm going to die regardless."

"We're a very long way from that," I said. "Particularly if you can tell us the truth."

I fell silent again, feeling that it was better to wait for her to decide to talk than to badger her into doing it. Eventually, my patience was rewarded.

"All right," she said at length. "I'll tell you."

"Go on…"

"My fiancé. His name is Major Robert Walker. He works for British Intelligence."

I glanced across at the Marx Brothers, who seemed to have perked up at this information.

"He was sent to France … to do God knows what… He couldn't tell me, of course, but I knew it was top secret and dangerous…"

She paused once again, as if struggling with her emotions. There was something she was finding difficult to deal with, I could tell that much.

"I heard recently, unofficially, that … he'd been captured by the Nazis … and … well, you know … all those things we were told about the Gestapo … they're probably going to do it to him…"

She put her head in her hands and started to sob almost uncontrollably. As much as I wanted to comfort her, I stayed put. Harpo was motioning me to stay sitting down. After a while, her sobs subsided and she looked up again, dashing the tears from her face.

"It's very likely, I suppose, that he'll be moved to that prison camp that we're going to bomb and…"

The penny dropped. Her motives suddenly became blindingly clear.

"You wanted to stop us from bombing it, is that right?"

"Yes, yes… I didn't want him to die… I didn't want to be part of killing him… I love him… I love him so much…"

She dissolved into tears once more. I let her cry it out. Once she had begun to tell the truth, her voice had seemed stronger, as if it was suddenly easier. I moved beside her and put my arm around her to comfort her. It was hard to imagine the pain she must have felt knowing that he was captured and would suffer a horrible fate at the hands of the Gestapo. My heart went out to her.

When she was finally more composed, I remained sitting next to her.

"You know," I said quietly, "that he's going to be killed anyway." There wasn't any easy way to say it.

"I know," she said. "I just didn't want to be a part of it."

"So, you thought that by sabotaging the planes, you'd stop us from carrying out the mission?"

"Yes … stupid of me, I know… I just couldn't bear to feel I'd been involved in his death… I'm sorry… I'm so sorry."

I wasn't sure what to do with this somewhat understandable reaction on her part, but I felt reasoning with her might be helpful.

"You didn't think that instead we'd try to find out who was doing it?"

"No … I didn't think at all, if I'm honest," she said, looking contrite.

"You didn't think that one of us might be killed because of your actions?"

She shook her head miserably. "I swear to you that I never thought about that. Now I see how reckless it was."

"You know that whether you took part in it or not, the mission would still go ahead," I continued, pressing the point. "It's too important."

Ruth said nothing. It was time for some unpalatable truths.

"It's hard for me to say this, but you would be doing your fiancé a disservice by letting him endure more than he has to. If you love him, as you say you do, then bombing the prison is for the best, for him and all of those who have been taken prisoner."

"I *do* love him," she said fiercely, as if I had doubted it.

"Then you have to do what's right. It's also your duty as a part of the Sirens. Think about it, Ruth: what would Robert say to you right now about this?" I asked her.

"He'd tell me to stop being a silly goose and get on with it," she said, laughing weakly.

"Exactly," I said.

"But it's too late now, for me … isn't it?" she said, becoming serious.

"I don't know," I replied.

An idea was forming in my mind, but it would require some persuasion to get James and the Marx Brothers to agree to it.

"Am I still going to … hang?" she asked in a small voice.

"Not if I have anything to do with it," I told her.

It seemed she had little faith in my ability to change her fate. I felt I had asked her enough to at least absolve her of spying. The Marx Brothers might well want more detailed information, however.

"You need to answer their questions," I told her, indicating the two spies. "If they want to ask you anything more, answer them truthfully."

"Yes, all right," she said.

I smiled at her in what I hoped was a reassuring way and stood up. The Marx Brothers came over to the table and spent another half hour interrogating her about Robert and her part in the sabotage. When they were satisfied, we left Ruth in the room and convened once more in the corridor.

"It so happens we know Major Walker," said Harpo. "Should have recognised her sooner as his fiancée."

"So, you don't think she's a spy?" I asked them.

"No, it looks like you hit the nail on the head."

"We should get you to do more of these interrogations," said Chico. "You're rather good at it."

"I'd rather not," I replied seriously.

"No … well, never mind. The question remains: what should we do with her now?" said Harpo.

"You're not going to hang her?" I said, concerned.

"No, she's not a traitor, but bloody stupid all the same," he replied, taking a drag on his cigarette.

I decided to float my idea and see how it landed. "What if I could persuade her to still fly the mission?"

"You jest, surely?" said Chico.

"Her reliability and loyalty to the Sirens is already in question," said Harpo.

"Yes, I know," I said. "But can't people redeem themselves?"

"She belongs in prison," said Harpo. "At least for the rest of the war, to put her out of harm's way."

"That just seems a tragic waste of a good pilot," I said.

The Marx Brothers shrugged, as if it was of no consequence.

"Why don't we see what James has to say about it? Whatever he decides, I'll abide by it," I suggested.

"All right," said Harpo. "But I wouldn't hold out much hope that he'll do anything but agree that she needs locking up."

"We'll see, won't we?" I replied.

"We will indeed," said Chico.

James heard me out in silence as I explained what had transpired with Ruth. Then he listened carefully to the Marx Brothers telling him why they thought Ruth should go to prison.

"All right, and what's your opinion, Anna? I take it that you don't agree with our colleagues here from MI6," he said.

"Part of me does," I replied truthfully. "But the bigger part of me says that we need her."

"Go on," he said.

"If we are to do maximum damage to that Nazi prison, we need every plane we can get. One less plane means less bombs. If you put her in prison, you've effectively grounded one plane and we'll only be going in with eleven."

"And you might jeopardise the success of the whole mission and all twelve planes if you to take her," said Harpo.

"Let her finish," said James patiently. "You've had your say. I want to hear Anna's reasoning."

Harpo didn't demur but instead lit up another cigarette to replace the one he'd just finished.

"I understand how you all feel about this," I said. "I'm not putting myself forward as a great judge of character, but all the same I can't see that there was any other motive for what she did than she's told us."

"But can she be trusted?" James asked me.

I warmed a little to my theme, gaining confidence in what I was proposing. "She knows that we know it was her sabotaging the planes; it seems highly unlikely she would do it again. Besides, wouldn't it be prudent to have them guarded at night instead of leaving them unattended?"

He smiled at me encouragingly. "You have a point there, regardless of whether she's been caught. It has proven that they are vulnerable. I should have thought of it before."

"Isn't it better to take the risk and have a full squadron attack, rather than go with even one less plane? You've told us all how important this mission is," I continued.

"What if she can't do it, when it comes to it?" he said. "What if she doesn't drop the bombs after all? Then you may as well not have taken her at all."

The Marx Brothers looked on approvingly at these words, which no doubt echoed their own sentiments. I began to wonder if James had made his mind up and if I was fighting a losing battle. Nevertheless, I persisted.

"Then she'd be disobeying direct orders. I don't think she would do that. But why don't you talk to her?" I asked him. "See for yourself if you think she's up for it. If you think she might be, then why not let her practise with us? Then if one thing goes wrong, ground her, imprison her, or do what you want with her. If not, then let her fly the mission."

James regarded me thoughtfully. "Let her prove herself, is that what you're suggesting?"

"Something like that, yes."

He raised another point. "There is the matter of all your friends who also know what she's done. Can they be relied upon to keep quiet? If this gets out, then I've no option but to have her incarcerated."

I considered this for a few moments. I had told them not to say anything, which should have been enough to prevent them from doing so out of loyalty to me, if nothing else. I could imagine that some of them wouldn't like Ruth flying with us again. If it came to it, they would just have to put up with it.

"I don't think they will have said anything, sir, no. I asked them not to," I told him.

James addressed himself to the Marx Brothers again. "Are the two of you still vehemently opposed, now you've heard Anna out?"

Harpo took a drag on his cigarette and shrugged. "It's your decision, old man. Whatever it is, we'll abide by it."

I took that as tacit consent and James seemed of the same mind.

"All right," he said. "Perhaps you'd like to get Ruth and bring her here. I will talk to her and make a final decision."

The Marx Brothers left the room. While they were gone, James said quietly, "Why does this matter to you so much, Anna?"

"Because sometimes people deserve a second chance," I replied at once, "particularly if they've done something very foolish."

"Was it *just* foolish?" he said, raising that quizzical eyebrow to devastating effect once more.

"In her case, I believe so, yes," I said, ignoring the flutter in my stomach.

"I'm inclined to agree," he told me. "I trust your judgement."

Somehow, the fact he'd said that was incredibly important to me. I wanted to hear he had faith in me.

The Marx Brothers returned in short order with Ruth in tow. She snapped to attention at once in James's presence and saluted.

"At ease, Ruth," he said. "Sit down for a moment."

She complied and sat eyeing him with some misgiving, as if he was a judge about to deliver a verdict.

"Ruth," he said, "supposing I was to let you fly with the squadron again, would you be willing or even able to carry about the mission we've been tasked with?"

Ruth nodded at once. "Yes, sir, and … I'm sorry, sir, for all of the trouble I've caused. I feel terribly ashamed of my actions." She sounded genuinely contrite, which was encouraging.

"So, if you were to be allowed to continue flying with the Sirens, would I have your word that you would never jeopardise the squadron or any mission again? That you would faithfully carry out your duty, no matter what the cost?"

"Yes, sir," she said.

"In which case, I'm giving you a choice: you can continue as a pilot, or find yourself being court-martialled," James said. "And you can thank Flight Officer Nightingale, because without her powers of persuasion you would almost certainly end up headed for a military prison."

He sounded very serious. She could be in no doubt of his resolve if she were to fail the Sirens again.

"Sir, I want to fly, please. I'm ready to fly," she said.

"Very well," James told her. "You can fly on the condition that you keep your word. If any hint of you not having done so reaches my ears, then you will most certainly never fly with the Sirens again."

He didn't need to add the additional consequences she would likely face.

"Thank you, sir," she said. "And thank you, Flight Officer Nightingale."

"It's quite all right," I said. "Just do your duty from now on."

"I will, I promise you that. I won't let you down again," she said.

"You are dismissed, Ruth, and you are never to speak to anyone about this outside of the five of us here, understood?" said James in a kindlier tone than he had used before.

"Yes, sir, thank you." She saluted once more, turned smartly on her heel and left.

"Right then, now that's dealt with, bring your motley crew up here, Anna, so that I can read them the riot act," James told me.

I went away to comply. He evidently knew that they were a bunch of strong characters. However, I didn't doubt his capacity to deal with them.

I rounded up the others and they accompanied me back to the office, annoyed that I refused to answer their questions as to what it was about. Once inside, we stood in a line.

"At ease, all of you," said James affably. "I know you've all done an excellent job regarding the saboteur, and I want to thank you for that. However, there's a mission to fly, and sometimes the greater good needs to prevail."

"You're not going to let her fly, are you…?" Shelly blurted out, trailing off as she caught James's expression.

"Did I invite you to speak, ASO Cartwright?" he asked her in a deceptively mild tone.

"No, sir."

"Then, I suggest you wait until I do," he told her.

Shelly blushed scarlet and didn't reply. James could certainly be commanding when he wanted to.

"All right," he continued. "Listen very carefully. You can never tell anyone what has transpired outside of this group as regards Section Officer Ruth Maddison, understood?"

"Yes, sir," came the immediate response. Nobody else wanted to become a target for his disapproval.

"I do mean *anyone*!" he said firmly. "I've come to a decision after consulting with your Flight Leader and the gentlemen from MI6. SO Maddison will continue to fly with the squadron and *will* fly the mission. Anna, here, will explain the reasoning behind it and Ruth's motives for doing what she did."

I spent a few minutes telling them what had transpired regarding Ruth, because I felt they deserved to know the truth. I explained why I felt she should fly. Nobody said anything, although I could tell from one or two expressions that I didn't entirely have their endorsement. I realised that didn't matter: I was the Flight Leader, and it was my decision.

When I had finished, James said, "Now you've heard what Anna has to say. If any of you wish to take the matter up with me, step forward now and we'll do so."

Predictably, nobody wanted to tangle with the CO, so they all remained silently in place.

"All right, then that's an end to it," he said. "You've got a mission to fly, and that's what you need to focus on, nothing else. Got it?"

"Yes, sir," was the unanimous response.

"You're all dismissed," he said quietly.

We saluted and left his office. As we were walking down the corridor, Shelly piped up.

"What were you thinking, Anna?" she said a little heatedly.

Ordinarily I would have engaged with this because we were all friends. However, I realised that being in a position of command also sometimes set one apart by necessity. This was one of those times. I stopped abruptly and turned to face her.

"Shelly and anyone else, we are not going to discuss this. I told you my reasons in there and that's an end to it. We'll say no more — that's an order," I said, bristling a little and daring any of them to defy me.

Instead, Maria came to stand beside me. "You heard the boss," she said. "She's made her decision. So you can shut it and put up with it."

"Blimey O'Reilly, Anna's on the warpath now. You lot had better watch out," said Patricia.

It broke the ice and we all burst out laughing. Shelly relented. She came up and gave me a hug.

"Sorry, Boss," she said. "I'll be good from now on."

"You're incorrigible, Shelly," I told her.

"That's what her mother used to say," said Maria. "And she wasn't wrong."

"Well, I think all this calls for a drink later," said Jennifer. "And a toast to my big sister, leader of the pack."

"What kind of pack are we, though?" said Pamela.

"A pack of witches, according to Gary," put in Susan.

We started laughing all over again. In perfect harmony once more, we made our way back to my room. I realised I probably now had a new nickname. Henceforth it was highly likely I'd be referred to as 'Boss'. Funnily enough, I quite liked it.

CHAPTER TWENTY

The hiatus due to the sabotage was now over, and the actions of preparing for the second mission began. James held a briefing which marked the start of the serious business which would lead up to bombing the prison. Once more James, Henry, Gloria and the Marx Brothers were standing on the podium in the briefing room, addressing us all.

"Operation Crossfire, the codename for the mission to destroy the Carlingue prison, will take place within a short space of time. The exact timing of it is not currently known," said James. "However, in order to prepare for it, we are making some additions to two of the aircraft in the squadron. Henry will brief you on this development."

Henry stepped forward and began to speak. "Two of the Mosquitos are to be fitted with new Mk. VIIIA radar. This radar will enable you to detect airborne threats at a distance. Since the mission will be flown at night, this will be an advantage in avoiding Jerry night fighters who may be patrolling the airspace near or around the prison, or indeed on the flight path into it."

I wondered whose planes were to be fitted with the devices, but Henry answered that in the next moment.

"The radar will entail removal of the four Browning machine guns in the nose area, leaving the cannons only in the belly. The Mosquitos will still carry a payload of bombs. A thimble nose will be fitted over the radar receiver. Although this will put those planes at a disadvantage with regards to armaments, it will put the squadron at a superior advantage which outweighs that. Flight Officer Nightingale will make an operational decision as to which planes in the squadron will receive the radar units. Those two crews will have special training on how to use them."

Quite a few eyes immediately swivelled to me. Since this was the first I'd heard of it, I knew I would have to think carefully regarding the right crews to operate the units. I kept my gaze to the front, avoiding the looks from my friends. I had no doubt some of them would put a bid in for the privilege.

"Thank you, Henry," said James. "We will undertake daytime and nighttime practice runs. A dummy target will be marked out on the range so that you can rehearse the attack. Remember that we cannot afford for this to fail. We have to be ready to go the moment we hear that the prisoners are being transferred to the new facility."

The Marx Brothers, who had been quietly smoking cigarettes in the background, now stepped up to speak.

"Intelligence reports have told us that the prison is nearing completion. It's perhaps a matter of days, or a few weeks at the outside. Reconnaissance photographs will be taken as close as possible to it being finished," said Harpo.

"Once we have the green light, then Operation Crossfire will spring into action. You need to study the photographs carefully and also those of the route in beforehand. These will all be available here in what is also now the operations room for this mission," said Chico.

"Full briefing orders will be given out just before the mission, including route, bearings, timings, codenames, and so forth," said Harpo.

"All right," added James. "For today let's get back in the saddle, so to speak, and run a low flying exercise. The Mosquitos have all been declared airworthy, and we don't anticipate any further problems with them."

He looked directly at me when he said this. We both knew what the other was thinking. Only a few members of the Sirens knew what had really transpired. I shot a few glances at Ruth, but she kept her eyes firmly on the floor.

"All right," said James. "Dismissed, let's get to it."

As we filed out to get into our flying gear, I made my way over to Ruth. She looked up as I stood in front of her.

"Before you say anything," she said, "I gave you my word and I'm keeping it."

"Thank you," I replied, relieved. Sometimes people had second thoughts, and we couldn't afford that now.

"No," she said. "Thank *you*, for giving me another chance."

"It's all right," I said, lightly touching her arm. "I believe in you."

She smiled, then got up from her chair and left.

"She'd better keep her promise," Maria growled in my ear. She had been standing beside me unnoticed during this exchange.

"She will," I said to her. "I'm sure of it."

I came to a decision about one of the radars almost immediately on leaving the briefing. I caught up to Jennifer and pulled her aside.

"What is it?" she asked.

"Jenny," I said, "I would like your plane to take one of the radars."

She looked surprised. "Why me?"

"Because I know I can rely on you implicitly."

It was true. I knew I could always count on her. Perhaps it was because we were related, but I also found I was thinking more like a leader. I was learning from James and Henry without even realising it.

"You say the nicest things, and not just because I'm your sister," she said, smiling.

"Who else do you think I should choose?" I asked her.

She thought for a moment. "What about Linda?"

I valued her opinion, but her answer surprised me.

"Linda? Are you serious?"

"Maybe giving her that level of responsibility might be helpful."

"It will be helpful if she is going to do a decent job," I said. "Not just to mollify her."

"Oh, I see … well, why don't you ask her?" suggested Jennifer.

Linda's disloyalty still rankled. Though she had not sabotaged the planes, she had been actively undermining my position before James had spoken to her. I had not quite forgiven her for that. There was also the possibility she might throw the offer in my face, like she had when I'd put her in charge of Beta Team on the previous mission. I wasn't prepared to look like a fool either.

"No," I said with resolution. "I'll ask Susan. I can rely on her too."

"All right, Boss, as you wish," Jennifer replied at once.

I sighed. Now even my sister was calling me 'Boss'. Soon they would be all doing it.

As we wound up the planes ready for action and I called the flight to check in, the answers came back almost invariably the same.

"Bluebird Two ready, Boss."

"Bluebird Three ready, Boss."

All except Bluebird Seven, SO Linda Harris. My feelings about not asking her to take one of the radars were thus confirmed. Subdued she may have been by James, but I had the notion she would always be my enemy deep down because of what she believed I had stolen from her. In her eyes, she was the obvious choice for leader and nothing anyone could say would change that. Yet leadership had been thrust upon me; I had not asked for it. Now I had it, though, I found myself wanting to keep it. It was fulfilling in a way I had never imagined. At the same time, I had never expected to have to watch my back because of a colleague, and yet here I was doing it. Fortunately, I had almost all the rest of the squadron watching it too.

Susan had accepted the offer to fly with the radar graciously and said she'd do her very best. Pamela would be the one operating the radar, as would Shelly in Jennifer's plane. It was good to resume flying practice and we once more slipped into the routine.

Jennifer, Shelly, Susan and Pamela received special training with the radar. They went up as a pair, with Henry flying a Spitfire. They had to find his plane using the radar in the daytime and then at night. Once they became proficient, the whole squadron flew with radar planes, repeating the exercise. This required close coordination between me, Maria, Shelly and Pamela. Once we contacted the Spitfire on the radar, I had to turn the whole squadron and outrun him, over and over again.

All of us knew the day would come when we would get the call. It arrived sooner than most of us expected. We found ourselves sitting the briefing room once more when James made the announcement.

"The transfer of prisoners is imminent," he said. "In fact, we expect to get the green light in three days' time or less. That gives you only a little more time to prepare. Your main focus now will be to rehearse the bombing and familiarise yourself with the terrain. Be prepared to go at short notice."

Harpo stepped forward then and motioned for the lights to be dimmed. The projector came on and a slide was seen of the prison complex. It consisted of a barbed wire fencing perimeter surrounding what looked like a concrete wall. There was one gate in and out. Then there were several buildings within and one main building all on one level.

"This is the Carlingue secret prison," said Harpo. "You will need to study the photographs carefully. Our intelligence suggests that the prisoners will be kept in these buildings here which consist of prison cells. The main interrogation building is this. These are the barracks for the soldiers and interrogators."

He indicated each set in turn with a pointer.

"The primary target is the prison cells. The secondary target is the barracks. If you can destroy their infernal interrogation rooms at the same time, then that would be even better."

I glanced over at Ruth to see if there was any reaction from her, but she was stony-faced. The buildings were not close together but spread out. Perhaps this was deliberate, since they might expect a bombing raid from the air. More photographs were shown, this time taken on the ground.

"One of our operatives risked their life to get these pictures," said Chico. "You can see from the outside that the signs clearly discourage anyone stopping by. The area between the barbed wire and the wall is mined. The locals are under the impression that it's a scientific research laboratory. I suppose you might be able to draw that analogy, given its real purpose."

It was a dry, sardonic comment which drew no laughter. We had some idea of the grim deeds which would take place within, were it allowed to stand. I was determined it would not. We would do our best to bomb the place to hell.

The lights went up, and Henry raised the projection screen to reveal the map underneath.

"The flight will take off at around midnight," he said, "proceeding at low level to the east of London, crossing the Thames at East Tilbury. Then it will continue down to Eastbourne, where you will leave the British coast."

He paused for a moment, drawing the pointer down the route which had been carefully indicated in red. It was set to keep us over the rural landscape as much as possible.

"Once you are over the Channel, you will fly just above wave height until you hit the French Coast. You will cross the coastline just east of Saint-Valery-en-Caux and then continue to a small village called Saint-Antoine. Just on the outskirts of this is the prison."

He went on to describe the method of attack. I tried to visualise it in my head as he was speaking.

"For the attack run, you will spread the squadron into two lines of six, one behind the other. The first line will drop their ordnance and the second will fly over that and drop theirs. The ordnance will be on timed fuses to allow you to get clear. Once you've done it, get the hell out. There are watch towers with machine guns; you may find it necessary to neutralise these on the way in if you are spotted. I doubt the ack-ack will be an issue, because you will be too low for them and you'll be gone before they can deploy it properly."

There was silence as the reality hit us once more. We'd flown one mission, but even so, the possibility of being killed in action was inescapable.

James then spoke very quietly and calmly. "This is what you've all trained for," he said. "Just follow your training and do what you do. Don't think about anything but the target and coming home safely. Keep focused, keep alert and you'll come through it."

I was in a sober mood as the briefing finished. The distance to the target was around three hundred miles as the crow flies. A bit further, due to our route. It was well within our capabilities and the operational distance of the aircraft. It would, however, be three hundred miles of adrenaline rush as we flew at low-level in the dark. I didn't relish the thought. I was particularly pensive at our lunch table.

"We'll be fine, Boss," said Shelly, as if she was reading my mind.

"Yes," I said. "We will."

"We will," added Maria.

"Yes," said Connie. "Because we are the Sirens."

We flew two rehearsals, one in the day and one at night. The ground on the range had been marked out as close to the layout of the prison as possible. The second time we used live ordnance. After that, I felt we were more than ready. In fact, in a way I couldn't wait for the moment to come, so that we could get it over with.

The morning after our final practice run, a briefing was called. There was an atmosphere of suppressed excitement. James and the others on the podium seemed to sense our mood. I could tell from his demeanour that he had news that was out of the ordinary. When he stepped forward to speak, he seemed a little tense, not his usual phlegmatic self.

"Sirens," he said. "This is it. Tonight is the night. Operation Crossfire is green to go."

Though I'd been anticipating it, I could not suppress the feeling of anxiety that went with the news. The mission was on, and it was down to me to ensure its success. My heart began to beat a little faster. On paper, it was a straight run to drop some bombs and come home. The reality was somewhat different. Flying a live mission, as I had already discovered, was nothing like practice. I put my attention back on James; he was still talking.

"It goes without saying that we're counting on all of you to do your duty. I could give you a speech about that and what this all means, but you already know it. Instead, let me just tell you this. Get the job done, but please come back. Do your damndest, because no matter what happens tonight, I'm so damn proud of you all. This isn't just *any* squadron. This is the Sirens. We are all of us part of something special. Never forget it, as I'll never forget each and every one of you and what you've achieved, becoming the fighting force you are."

He was looking directly at me when he said it. I choked up inside.

The Marx Brothers seemed to have lost their usual laconic demeanour and even temporarily abandoned their cigarettes. Harpo spoke in a passionate tone I'd rarely heard from him.

"I just want you to know that this also isn't just *any* mission. The success of it has far-reaching consequences — secrets and lives preserved well beyond those you are about to take. The secret war in Europe depends on it. So good luck and Godspeed."

"What he said," Chico chimed in.

We all laughed as his quip broke the tension in the room. Then Gloria and Henry also wished us well. With the formalities over, we went back to studying the briefing sheets, photographs and the maps. I tried to imprint the pictures on my mind, knowing that at night it would be very different. We were all relying on dead reckoning and on Maria most of all as the lead navigator.

The clock wound around to dinner. My group sat around our usual table together, eating pie, mash and cabbage.

"You'd think we could have had steak or something for our last meal," said Connie.

"I sincerely hope this *isn't* our last meal," said Pamela.

"I don't know about the rest of you," said Jennifer, "but I'm coming back, and so is my sister."

I smiled at this. She always had been my biggest cheerleader as much as I'd been hers.

"Well," said Shelly, "I've written my will, such as it is. You'll find it on the desk in my room."

"Oh, gosh," said Susan. "I hadn't thought of that. Maybe I should write mine."

This talk was more than I could bear.

"Enough," I said. "Stop talking as if we're going to the scaffold, all of you. We're carrying out this mission and we're coming back, understood? We're coming back because we are needed to fly more missions after that and because I said so, all right?"

The others giggled at my sudden assertive tone. It broke the despondent mood.

"The Boss has spoken," said Maria. "Now shut up, the lot of you, and eat. You can't fly a mission on an empty stomach."

"Don't tell me," said Shelly sarcastically. "That's what your mother used to say."

"No, she didn't, you idiot," Maria replied, laughing. "She wasn't flying bloody missions, for a start."

I shook my head and addressed myself to my pie. After dinner, most of us went to our rooms to while away the time or catch some sleep until it was time to fly. I lay down for a while too and slept fitfully. Jennifer had not come back with me. I presumed she was out somewhere with Connie.

When I awoke, it was around nine p.m. The room was dark. I got up to go to the window. Outside, the formal gardens were bathed in moonlight. I wondered if it would hold and make our flight a little easier. A movement caught my eye; it was Jennifer and Connie, walking together and holding hands. They often strolled together in the gardens, so that was unremarkable, but this time seemed different. Jennifer suddenly turned to Connie. Connie's arms slid around her neck. Their lips met in a kiss.

I looked away, feeling that I had intruded upon something which perhaps I should not. When I turned back again a few moments later, they were gone.

I turned on the bedside lamp and started to check through my flying gear when Jennifer came into the room. She looked a little flushed and bright-eyed.

"Jenny…" I began, wanting to tell her I knew, because we didn't keep secrets as sisters. I should have guessed it a lot sooner.

But she stopped me. "Anna, please don't say anything," she replied, as if reading my mind. "I love her and she loves me."

I remembered a conversation during which she'd once told me that when I found love, it would be the most glorious thing I'd ever felt. Now I knew who she was referring to.

I sighed. "All right."

"Don't sigh like that," she said. "We're going on a mission. Either or both of us might be killed."

I got up and hugged her tight. "Don't say that," I whispered. "Don't think like that, Jenny."

"It's the truth," she said softly.

I pulled away from her a little without letting her go and said seriously, "All right, Jenny, but you know, we promised each other we wouldn't die."

"Connie might die…" she said, trailing off.

"She won't," I said, hugging her again.

She shuddered on a sob for a moment. I held her close until she felt better. In the end, she was right. Any of us might not make it back, and who was I to judge? Perhaps it was a conversation for another time, but today was not that day.

We said no more, and I put it from my mind. It was, after all, none of my business who Jennifer chose to love. There was a mission to fly. We needed to focus on the task ahead. I wished that we had phoned our parents that evening, but I could never tell them we were flying into danger. We rang them quite often, lying through our teeth about the planes we were supposedly transporting all over England. They would never know the truth, even if we didn't come back.

When the hour arrived, I helped Jennifer put on her flying gear and she helped me in turn. We did our final checks to make sure we'd got everything. Henry had made sure that everyone had once more been issued with grenades, and also that we still had the pills which we had kept from the previous mission. Right on cue, there was a soft knock at the door. It was Maria and the others.

"All set, Boss?" she said.

"As I'll ever be," I replied, smiling.

The corridors were silent as we walked downstairs, through the entrance hall and out to the waiting trucks. The others made me go first, along with Maria, our lead navigator. The night was crisp and cold, waking me up.

"Ooh, it's bloody freezing," complained Connie.

I was glad of the sheepskin jacket, which gave some semblance of warmth. As I got to the back of one of the trucks, James stepped out of the shadows, almost making me jump.

"Anna," he said, drawing me slightly aside.

The others started to climb up into the trucks while I stared at him.

"James," I said in surprise, forgetting protocol in the moment. My stomach was doing flips, just as it always seemed to when he was close.

"I just wanted…" He hesitated. It felt as if there was something he really needed to tell me, but instead he just said, "To wish you good luck."

"Thanks," I told him.

"Come back safe," he said quietly. "If you would."

"I'll do my best," I said, nodding. "I'd better get on."

"Of course," he said with a smile.

He watched me climb into the truck and take a seat next to Maria.

"Good luck, Sirens," he said.

"Thank you, sir," came the chorus of replies.

The trucks pulled away and he remained watching us until he was swallowed up by the gloom. Jennifer and Connie were sitting together in the back, sharing a last cigarette.

"Here we go then," said Shelly. "What say you? Are we going to get this done?"

"Damn right we are," said Patricia.

"Watch out, Jerry, because the Sirens are coming," Pamela added.

Suddenly, Maria burst into song. It was an old song from the Great War. "Keep the home fires burning, while your hearts are yearning, though we may be far away, we dream of home…"

Nearly all of us knew the words and we joined in, singing lustily and loudly all the way to the airfield. I felt something stirring in my breast. A feeling of courage, of togetherness; we were the Sirens singing our Siren song. As the trucks pulled up to the planes, we all whooped and cheered, disembarking in high spirits.

Victoria was there to meet us.

"Everything's been checked and triple-checked, ma'am," she said to me, snapping a salute. "You're all set to go."

"Thanks, Victoria," I said. "You're a treasure."

"Ma'am," she replied, smiling at the unexpected compliment.

I turned to the others, who were all waiting for the orders. "All right, Sirens, let's get this bloody job done!"

"Yes, Boss!" they shouted back.

Then we were striding out to the planes.

"Good luck, ma'am," Victoria called out to me. "Give my regards to Jerry."

I waved and laughed, climbing into the Mosquito in a buoyant mood. We started to go through the preflight checks. Then I fired up the engines and flicked on the navigation lights.

"Are you ready for this?" said Maria.

"Yes, are you?"

"Hell, yes," she said.

"Don't tell me," I quipped. "You were born ready."

"Not quite," she laughed. "But I'm ready now … as I'll ever be."

"Panthers check in," I said and waited for the responses.

"Panther Two ready, Boss."

"Panther Three ready, Boss."

I wondered who had chosen the codename. I rather liked it. It gave the impression of sleek black cats stealing through the night, hunting their prey. We were certainly going hunting.

"Control, this is Panther Leader requesting clearance," I said to the tower.

"You're clear to go," said Control. "Good luck, stay safe out there."

"Roger," I said, smiling.

"Panthers, let's go," I said, easing up the throttle. We taxied down to the end of the runway and I began to wind up the engines for take-off.

"Are we good?" I said to Maria.

"We're good," she said.

I let off the brakes and the Mosquito barrelled down the runway. We were airborne in moments and circling around for the rest of the flight. It was a clear night, and the moon was shining brightly. Perhaps it was an omen. The runway lights stayed on until the last plane left the ground and then they went off, leaving the airfield in darkness.

"Panthers form up, close formation, low level," I said.

Maria gave out the bearing and I steered us onto the heading.

"All right," I said. "Here we go, Panthers, it's showtime."

I dropped the Mosquito down to treetop height and opened up the throttle. Maria came alert at once. The routine kicked in without either of us needing to think.

"House."

"Yep, seen it."

"Treeline."

"Got it."

"Lines, lines, lines."

"Yes."

The ground flashed by at a tremendous pace, but we were used to it and to the darkness. My eyes quickly adjusted, able to make out features and obstacles. All the training had been vital to bring us to this point.

Jennifer and Shelly in Panther Four along with Susan and Pamela in Panther Six were the radar planes. They would be keeping a close eye on the radar in case of airborne contact.

We flew down to Chelmsford without incident, and then eased between Billericay and Brentwood. We crossed the Thames at East Tilbury, as dictated by the flight plan. The tide was in and the water shimmered in the moonlight. Chatham and Tunbridge Wells flashed by as we headed for the Downs and Eastbourne.

"Ever been there?" said Maria. "Tunbridge Wells?"

"I think maybe once," I replied.

"You were a real homebody, weren't you?"

"I suppose I was." I laughed.

"And look at you now ... and look out for those trees... Christ..."

I joined in with her laughter as I skimmed the treetops with inches to spare.

"Take it easy, Boss," she said. "I want to get to the target in one piece at least."

"Sorry..."

The downside of competence is that it can make you overconfident. I needed to rein that in. Maria was right. Besides, we were about to leave friendly shores. Anything could happen from here on in. A sudden thought occurred to me.

"I'll tell you what," I said. "If we get through this, let's all of us go to Tunbridge Wells."

"What?" she said, laughing again.

"It'll be fun, a Sirens outing."

"All right, you're on…"

I gained height to skim over the hills and then down again. Suddenly, there it was: Beachy Head. I'd been there too and seen the towering, majestic chalk cliffs. I had always wondered how it might be to fly off those cliffs like a bird. Now I was about to find out.

"Panthers, kill the lights," I said, flicking off the navigation lights. "Radars on high alert."

"Roger," said Jennifer and Susan.

"Panthers, here we go, all the way to the Big Top."

The Big Top was the codename for the Carlingue Prison. The prison we were going to take down. I tried to imagine what it would be like to be someone being taken there, not knowing what fate awaited you but expecting something quite horrific, ending in death. We were simply bringing that ending sooner to our people. It had to be done; there wasn't a choice.

I dropped the flight down to wave height. The water was choppy but fortunately not too rough. Maria gave us a new heading to take us directly to Saint-Valery-en-Caux, where we would make landfall. The Channel was once more an inky black. We were so low that it seemed as if we were in touching distance of the water.

"Take it easy, Boss," said Maria, eyeing the surface of the sea with some misgiving. "I don't fancy a swim tonight."

"Don't worry. I don't fancy one either," I said, laughing.

I flicked a glance at her. She seemed unusually tense. The mission was affecting us all in different ways. I felt sharper and more focused than I ever had.

Every so often I'd check my wings and make sure that the black shapes of the other Mosquitos were still there. They were, of course, nice and tight in formation. On exercises there was usually a little more chatter, but now we had to maintain radio silence. Confident with the presence of the radar, I didn't scan the sky for Jerry planes; in any case, I doubted I would have seen them in the dark.

"Coastline dead ahead," said Maria, after what seemed an interminable time crossing the Channel.

"Got it."

Dark cliffs loomed up before us, overlooking the beach. I knew about these from the photographs and took us up higher. Crossing the French coastline had its dangers, apart from the cliffs, the main one being German coastal lookouts. Hopefully we wouldn't get spotted. It was always a risk.

Even if we did, though, we'd be gone before they could do anything about it. I held my breath for a moment, but we passed over the beach without incident. Then we were flying low over rural France. Flat fields, lines of trees and hedges abounded. The moon held up even here and bathed the landscape in its eerie light. Maria resumed her role as lookout.

"Trees."

"Got it."

"Lines, lines, lines."

"Yep, seen them."

"House."

"Yes."

She adjusted the bearing as we went. As I hadn't been schooled in navigation, I wasn't sure how she got things so dead on. To me she was a marvel; without her I'd be lost. My job was to fly the plane, and I was very good at that.

"How far now?" I asked her, thinking Saint-Antoine and the prison must be getting closer.

"Patience," she said softly, looking at her map.

I waited for her to tell me as the landscape flashed by.

"Halfway," she said at length. "Not long now."

My pulse began to race a little faster on hearing this. The moment of truth would soon arrive.

Suddenly the radio crackled to life.

"This is Panther Six, radar contact on our nine o'clock," said Pamela.

This was not good news.

"How many?" I said at once.

"Looks like one bandit, heading towards us," Pamela replied.

"Confirmed," said Shelly, who would have picked it up on the other radar.

There was nothing for it but to see what transpired.

"Panthers stay on course," I said. "Keep me informed, Six and Four."

"Wilco," came the response.

Maria looked over at me with a quizzical expression.

"What can we do?" I said to her. "It's probably higher than us, and if we're lucky it won't see us."

"And if it does?"

"We'll deal with it if that happens," I told her.

We both knew there wasn't any choice other than to continue. Besides that, we had no idea if the aircraft was friend or foe. One Jerry fighter could still hurt us very badly, if we were spotted. We just had to hope we were not.

Tense minutes went by as I put my attention back on the objective. Just as I was wondering whether or not the plane was going to intercept us, Pamela radioed again.

"Bandit now heading away from us," she said.

"Confirmed," added Shelly.

"Roger," I replied.

"That's a bloody relief," said Maria with a nervous laugh.

"Let's hope there are no more," I said, glad that nothing untoward had occurred after all.

"Amen to that. Oh, and we're getting close. We'll soon be on the approach."

Maria changed the bearing, and moments later we were flying just abreast of a country road. We came to a junction and with another new bearing turned due south.

"This is the road in," she said, indicating the one we were following. "We should hit the target in ten."

"Well, this is what we came for," I said.

I mentally prepared myself for the final moments. I waited as the minutes ticked by, watching the road slipping past below us.

"In five," said Maria.

This was it. I knew what to do. We'd rehearsed it more than once.

"Panthers attack formation, Big Top in five," I said, giving the order.

The flight split into two groups, three planes in front and three behind in each group. We spread out at the prearranged distance from each other. I remained in the middle of the formation at the front. I slipped off the safety on the guns and readied the bomb bay.

"Target should be coming up," said Maria. "Assuming I'm right."

I gave a hollow laugh. "You're always right," I said.

Then, suddenly, there was the prison, exactly as we'd seen it in the photographs. The perimeter was lit up by floodlights and the watch towers stood out starkly against the black sky.

"Panthers, ready, on my mark, engage incoming fire at will," I said, feeling the adrenaline beginning to course through my veins.

My heart began to thump as we flew towards the prison. All my attention was on the target and what I had to do. There was no room for conscious thought.

"Almost there," said Maria.

"Incoming fire," said Susan as a stream of tracers erupted from one of the watch towers. We had been spotted, but luckily the tower was in my sights.

"Take the towers down," I said, pressing the trigger.

Cannons from more than one Mosquito spewed out tracers. The bullets ripped into the towers, silencing the machine guns. The top of one of the towers fell over.

Then we were past them and across the wall. Beneath us we caught a glimpse of the ensuing mayhem. People were running about, but it was too late for any of them. We were over the target zone. It was time.

"Panthers, bombs away," I said, releasing our deadly payload.

As the bombs from twelve Mosquitos flew towards their intended target, we had seconds to get clear.

"Panthers out, get the hell out," I said, throttling up and banking sharply away as we crossed the far perimeter wall.

"Here's hoping we're on target," said Maria.

Ruth's voice suddenly cut in over the top of her. "Damn, damn it, damn, I hit the tower! I've hit the tower!"

"Panthers, keep going. Get clear," I said without missing a beat. Months of training had left their mark. "Panther Eight, what's your status?"

"I can't… I'm sorry… We won't make it… We're going back in… It's the only way," said Ruth.

"Damn, damn, damn," I swore as we pulled away from the prison.

I felt Maria's hand on my arm. "Get us out of here, Anna," she said. "You can't do anything about it."

"I know," I said. I didn't need reminding, not this time. "Just give me the bearing."

We banked around to go due north with the prison on our left-hand side. Just then, the bombs went off. There was a massive series of explosions and in the light from the flames, I clearly saw the silhouette of a Mosquito dropping into the inferno.

"Sorry, Panthers, we won't be coming with you… Brenda says goodbye…" It was the last thing we heard from Ruth before her plane disappeared into the raging fires we had left behind.

"Bearing zero one zero," said Maria, giving us the course.

"Let's go, Panthers, form up," I said, watching the planes settling on my wings.

I opened up the throttle, dropped down low and we were away. Behind us, the fires burned brightly. I hoped we'd done the damage we needed to do. There was no hanging around to find out. We had to get away before Jerry scrambled some night fighters to try and find us. Hopefully we'd be long gone if they did.

The way home seemed quicker than the way there. Perhaps it was the relief at a job well done. The darkness was somehow comforting as we made our escape. What had James told us? We'd be a deadly strike force, attacking by stealth. We'd certainly lived up to it.

"Not long to the coast," said Maria.

Just then, Shelly came on the radio.

"Radar contact dead ahead," she said.

"How many?" I asked at once.

"Hard to say, several bandits," she replied.

"We're closing the distance fast," said Pamela.

I looked at Maria and she looked at me. Our orders were to keep clear of enemy planes.

"We should go round them, shouldn't we?" she said.

"Yes…" I hesitated. "But they don't know we're coming."

"No," she said.

We both knew exactly what the other was thinking.

"Panthers, who's got ammo?" I asked the others.

The replies came back affirmative as the landscape continued to slip past below us.

"We'll be in visual contact in minutes if we don't change course, Boss," said Shelly.

I came to a decision, foolish or not. "Panthers," I said, "stay on course and prepare to engage. What height are the bandits?"

Shelly came back with the answer. They were higher than us, and we were fast coming up on them.

"What are you doing?" said Maria, although she knew full well.

"I'm in the mood to take them down," I told her.

"You're the boss."

I started to gain height. We'd attack them from underneath; that would be more effective, and they wouldn't see us.

"Panthers, you're clear to fire as soon as you have a clean shot," I said.

"Visual contact imminent," said Shelly. "We're close."

"We're on an intercept for sure," added Pamela, and then, "There are bandits at two o'clock high, just ahead."

We saw them, with moonlight glinting off their canopies. They were Jerry fighters for sure — I recognised the shape. We were behind them now, and they were moving away from us. They had their navigation lights on and were obviously not expecting us.

"You know we could just continue. They'd be none the wiser," said Maria.

"I know…" I said, going on the attack and opening up the throttle.

Then my whole attention was on my gunsight. I hoped the others were doing the same. The planes came into range very fast, and in seconds I had one in my sights. I fired the cannons and saw streams of tracers appear, streaking out from the Sirens squadron. Moments later, the bullets found their mark. Jerry planes were on fire and exploding in the sky.

I banked sharply and headed once more for the coast.

"Panthers, let's go, full throttle — go, go, go!" I said, unable to keep the jubilation out of my voice as we rapidly pulled away. Behind us, we left some fireballs and smoking planes diving to earth.

"Two in pursuit," said Shelly.

"Keep going," I said, feeling confident. "We'll outrun them."

"Roger, I'll keep tabs on them," she replied.

"Will we outrun them?" Maria asked me a little apprehensively.

"If I have anything to do with it, yes," I told her.

"Well … anyway … here's the coastline," said Maria.

I saw a brief flash of the cliffs and sand once more, then we were over the water.

"We're losing them," said Pamela.

"Roger," I replied.

"They're turning away," said Shelly.

This was good news. As confident as I might have felt, there was always an outside chance they might have caught up with us, but it was dark and they'd probably given up or lost sight of us.

"Roger," I said. "Panthers, let's get home."

I dropped the flight back down a little, but not too low, as we had to clear the cliffs at Beachy Head. Besides, the attack was over. The job was done.

"You sure as hell believe in making these missions exciting," said Maria, her familiar dry wit returning as we crossed over the English coast.

"I do my best," I said, laughing.

"One prison bombed and several planes to boot! What are you like?"

"I don't know what got into me, really," I said. That part was true. Perhaps it was the daredevil in me that saw my father berate me more than once in the past.

"You're certainly not the same shy Anna who I met that day in the dining room."

"No, I'm not."

"I'm glad," she said. "It needed to happen."

"Thank you," I said, smiling.

"I'm sorry about Ruth," she continued, becoming serious.

"It couldn't be helped, but it wasn't just Ruth, it was Brenda too," I said.

"Yes, I know."

There was nothing to be done. It was just bad luck, hitting that tower on the other side of the prison. Perhaps it was inattention. We would never know. Ruth was no longer there to ask.

We lapsed into silence, becoming a little more sombre. I dropped the flight low for the return journey and we made our way back to Hawberry. I felt sad about Ruth, but perhaps I'd started to get used to death. I didn't feel the same emotion as I had when Frances had died, nor the guilt. We'd done our duty and we'd done it well. We were probably fortunate to only lose one plane.

After some time, Hawberry hove into view and I was never gladder to see it.

"Control, this is Panther Leader requesting clearance to land," I said, suddenly feeling a little weary.

"Panther Leader, you're clear. We'll even put the lights on for you," Control replied, adding a little light-hearted quip.

"Roger and thanks."

The landing lights came on and I headed around the field for an approach. The rest of the squadron followed behind me.

"You got us home safely, that's what matters," said Maria.

"Thanks to you," I replied, knowing that her navigation was the key to our success.

She knew that too, but she was modest about it. I lowered the undercarriage and a few minutes later the wheels touched the ground.

"Woohoo!" cried Maria, regaining her good spirits. "We're home!"

"Yes," I said, relieved more than anything. "Home."

It was strange calling Hawberry home, but that's what it felt like because of the Sirens. We were a family now. I hoped it would always feel that way, even when the war was over.

I taxied the Mosquito to a stop and killed the engines. The two of us climbed down through the hatch using the ladder for a change, instead of jumping like we normally did. We were both feeling the fatigue that came after a mission.

"Hey, Boss, we did it!" said Shelly, coming up to me and giving me a hug.

"Yes, Shelly, we did."

"Hell yeah, we damn well gave Jerry one in the eye," said Connie, arriving too.

Then we were all whooping and hugging each other with the sheer joy of being back, after which we climbed into the waiting trucks and were soon on our way to Hawberry Hall.

"God, I needed that," said Connie, taking a grateful drag on a cigarette and passing it to Jennifer.

"Me too," said Jennifer.

"There'll be bluebirds over the white cliffs of Dover," sang Maria all of a sudden.

As a result, there was a spontaneous outburst of the familiar song as all of us joined in lustily until we arrived back at the Hall. As we jumped down from the trucks, the Marx Brothers, James, Henry and Gloria were there to greet us.

"Well done, Sirens, a bloody good job by all accounts," said Harpo with a grin.

"Yes, indeed, well done, absolutely marvellous," said Chico.

There was plenty of handshaking and congratulations before James bade us all go into the dining room for refreshments. I was about to follow the others when he stopped me.

"Stay a moment, Anna," he said.

"I'll catch you up," I said to Maria.

She shot me a sly look before leaving to join the group. Their voices faded into the distance as they went inside, and then we were alone. I looked at James and he was smiling at me.

"You know," he said, "you're not supposed to engage enemy aircraft. You're meant to run away from them."

"Yes," I said. "I know." My heart started to beat rather fast.

"Technically you disobeyed standing orders," he continued.

"I suppose technically, yes," I replied, locking eyes with him.

"Perhaps," he said softly as he closed the distance between us, "I ought to do something about it."

His lips were suddenly no more than an inch from mine. My heart was hammering in my chest. I couldn't tear my eyes away from him if I tried.

"Oh, and what are you going to about it, James?" I asked.

"What I should have done some time ago, if I'd only had the courage," he whispered.

To my immense relief, his lips found mine and I was lost. My arms snaked around his neck, pulling him into an embrace as fire began to course through my veins.

All my misgivings about him being my CO could go hang. At that moment, we were simply Anna and James. The future would have to take care of itself.

HISTORICAL NOTE

The history of women in combat goes back centuries. In Greek mythology, the Amazons were warrior women who fought in the Trojan War. There have been many famous female warriors throughout history, including the ancient British queen, Boudicca. Women fought on the front lines in the First World War for several Eastern European countries, including Maria Bochkareva, the founder of the Russian "Women's Battalion of Death". In the Soviet Union during the Second World War, women also served in aviation combat units, both as fighter and bomber pilots. Some were all-female units, one of the most well-known being nicknamed the "Night Witches". They also served in the Russian armed forces on the front lines: one of the most famous snipers of the war was Lyudmila Pavlichenko, who is credited with killing 309 Germans.

Women served on ack-ack batteries and barrage balloons in the Allied forces. Female pilots in the Air Transport Auxiliary also transported aircraft between factories and airfields across the UK. However, this has only recently come to light and has been the subject of documentaries and historical accounts. A similar role was performed by the WASPS in the US. That's not to mention all of the women who ably served in non-combat roles all over the UK. Since then, women have taken an increasingly prominent role in the Armed Forces across the world, both as combatants and non-combatants. Thus, history has set a precedent for the Sirens.

The de Havilland Mosquito was a multi-faceted combat aircraft which served in many different roles in the RAF. One of the most well-known of these were low-level strike missions into enemy territory. Mosquito squadrons flew as close to the ground as they could; they would skim over the Channel into France, Holland and other occupied countries to carry out daring bombing raids with great skill. It seemed to me the perfect plane for the Sirens, flying deadly stealth missions at night, striking the target with precision and, hopefully, coming home. Such flying has been described by pilots as terrifying, and it would require nerves of steel. The courage of those who flew these planes on such missions can never be diminished. I've tried to convey the sense of that in this series. Hopefully, I've succeeded.

If the Sirens had really existed, I like to think that they might have been very much like the heroines in my book.

A NOTE TO THE READER

Dear Reader,

I hope you enjoyed this book. It is something of a departure from my Spitfire Mavericks series, although the action still takes place during the Second World War. As I have said before, I like to explore the 'what-ifs' of history and place them within the context of the time.

In the case of the Sirens, the idea came following a discussion with my wife, who is a keen advocate of my writing. The premise was, what if British women had taken up a combat role in the war? What would that look like? How might it play out? It would of necessity have to be top secret, the best-kept secret of the war, if it had really happened.

The idea that the Sirens would be top secret naturally meant I had to think carefully about things like whether they could be captured if shot down, what would happen if they fraternised off the base and much more. I carefully considered all the options before taking what I felt was the most likely course of action or standing orders, given the scenario. While it is completely a work of fiction, I always endeavour to make my stories believable and entertaining. If I have succeeded, all well and good.

I also wanted to give the story a British angle. I opted for a Mosquito strike force because that was the most logical thing. It would be easily kept apart from other squadrons. Such strike squadrons did exist, although they were crewed by men. Above all, I've tried to convey the feeling of hope and determination to defeat the threat of Nazi domination, which was very much part of Britain in wartime: to do whatever it takes to get the job done, but with humour and sometimes grace.

I don't think there's anything incongruous about women going to war, and who knows, given that some of the most incredible secrets of the war are finally being revealed, perhaps something like the Sirens might have happened after all.

I hope you enjoyed reading this novel as much as I enjoyed writing it. If you did, then I would be very grateful if you could spare the time to write a review on **Amazon** and **Goodreads**. As an author, these reviews are hugely important, and always appreciated.

You can connect with me in other ways too, via my **website**, **Facebook**, **Twitter**, **Instagram**, and a special **Secret Sirens Page**.

I very much hope you were entertained enough to read the next book in the Sirens series.

Warmest regards

D. R. Bailey

Sapere Books is an exciting new publisher of brilliant fiction and popular history.

To find out more about our latest releases and our monthly bargain books visit our website: **saperebooks.com**

www.ingramcontent.com/pod-product-compliance
Lightning Source LLC
Chambersburg PA
CBHW070730280626
47159CB00023B/2973